John T. Trowbridge

Biding his Time

Andrew Hapnell's fortune

John T. Trowbridge

Biding his Time
Andrew Hapnell's fortune

ISBN/EAN: 9783337272319

Printed in Europe, USA, Canada, Australia, Japan

Cover: Foto ©Andreas Hilbeck / pixelio.de

More available books at **www.hansebooks.com**

"A CEREMONIOUS BOW FROM THE HAT AND CANE."   Page 38.

BIDING HIS TIME

OR

ANDREW HAPNELL'S FORTUNE

BY

J. T. TROWBRIDGE

———

BOSTON:
LOTHROP, LEE & SHEPARD CO.

CONTENTS.

ILLUSTRATIONS.

BIDING HIS TIME.

CHAPTER I.

HOW A POOR OHIO BOY HEARD OF A GREAT FORTUNE AWAITING HIM IN MASSACHUSETTS.

ANDREW HAPNELL'S mother had been two months dead, when one day he took from the post office a letter addressed to her, as if she had been still alive. It gave him a start to see the name once more on an envelope, passed out to him, as of old, from the little window; and it seemed to him for a moment that he was to hasten home and put it into her own dear hands. Then the recollection of his loss came over him like a black wave; and slipping the letter into his pocket, he walked sadly away.

Andrew was a boy of seventeen, — no longer a child nor yet a man, — "betwixt hay and grass," as the saying is. His mother had kept

9

him in school, and it had been her intention to
give him a good education; but since she had
died, and her pension with her (her husband,
a colonel of volunteers, had lost his life in the
war), the terrible question had stared the
orphan Andrew in the face, What was he
going to do?

He had thought of various things, and he
thought of them again now, as he walked home
to the house of his married sister, Mrs. Bateman, who gave him food and shelter in those
anxious days of waiting. Should he try to
work his way through college, and then struggle for a position in one of the crowded pro-
fessions? A most discouraging prospect! Or
should he give up that dream, and settle down
to some common occupation? He was willing
to do that if he could find the work which
seemed adapted to his taste and capacity; but
everything in his future was as yet bewildering
and uncertain.

He was a "good, faithful boy," as his mother
had always called him, grateful in her widow-
hood for so kind and helpful a son. He was

rather awkward in his manners, having long limbs and a shambling gait; and his slowness of speech almost amounted to a drawl. There was nothing very attractive in his appearance, unless you caught the expression of his sunny hazel eyes. They were about as earnest, honest, winning a pair, as ever softened and lighted up a homely face.

Thinking his sister, who was several years older than himself, the proper person to open the letter to their dead mother, he took it to her in the little dining-room, where she was setting the supper table, and put it into her hand. Then he sidled into a chair, in his awkward fashion, and watched to see her expression change as she read the superscription.

"Why! to mother!" she exclaimed, experiencing a sort of shock. Sinking down upon the nearest seat, she tore the envelope, glanced her eye over its contents, and as soon as she could get her voice, read aloud,—

Sister Jane: I take pen in hand to let you know I am yet in the land of the livving, and trust you are enjoying the same blesing. Would make you a visit, but the care of my

large propety keeps me here. Have been
prospered beyond expectations, and live in a
resdense truly palashal, overlooking Boston
and many other cities and towns, with servants
to comand.

As I am a bachler, and have no blood relations I care for, I wish you would come and
live with me and bring your famly, as there is
room for all, and grandchildren if you have
any, for I am a lonely old man with more of
this world's goods than I know what to do
with, and am anxus to use the same for your
benefit, remembring how kind your father was
to me. If you cannot all come, then send son
or dowter, which will provide for and edecate
and make my hair or hairess, as I wish none of
my blood to inherit of me. My millions is not
for such as them.

Sister Jane, I am ernest making this ofer,
and trust some if not all can axept, and soon.
Don't wait for me to write again, as it is very
difkilt for me to hold the pen. Will pay all
expences of jorney. Am well known here,
and easy found.

Your loving brother,
NATHAN PETRIDGE.

"Uncle Nathan!" exclaimed Mrs. Bateman,
in a sort of amused amazement, having finished
the scrawl, which was written in a cramped
hand, with a poor pen and faded ink, on a half

sheet of dingy letter paper. "I thought he was dead long ago.'

"I never knew I had such an uncle," said Andrew, with excited interest.

"You must have heard mother speak of him," she replied, while he reached for the letter and looked it over eagerly. "But he is not really our uncle. He lived in her father's family, a sort of adopted son. But he was always odd, and not very brotherly; and a good deal older than she was. After she married and moved to Ohio, one or two letters passed between them, and then they lost sight of each other. Now the idea of his turning up a millionaire, and inviting us all to go and share his riches! It takes my breath away."

"I remember now!" Andrew murmured, absorbed in thoughts which the strange letter aroused. "She told some funny stories about the things he would do to make money; and how he went barefoot after he got to be a young man, to save the cost of shoes. Well! he seems to have gone barefoot to some purpose! Wonder if he wears shoes now!"

They were still discussing the letter, when his brother-in-law came in; Andrew showed it to him and asked his opinion of it. George Bateman, a rough, brusque, good-humored man of forty, by trade a harness-maker, ran his stiff and blackened fingers through his hair, and replied with a laugh, —

"I think such an offer (with one f!) from an old bachelor with more money than he knows what to do with, ain't to be sneezed at! Of course, Laura and I can't accept it, but it's just the thing for you, Dan!"

"You think so?" said Andrew, with a flush of excitement. "It does seem strange that such a chance should be thrown in my way just at this time!"

"Let Dan go first," said Laura; "then if everything seems favorable we can pull up stakes here and follow him with the children."

"I expected that," laughed her husband. "You are not the woman to sit with hands folded, while 'resdenses truly palashal' are waiting for 'hairs' and 'hairesses' to walk in and take possession. But I shan't throw up my **business in** a hurry ; **and I** advise **Dan** to make pretty sure old Nate Petridge will do **by** him what he says, before he risks the journey."

Laura deemed this counsel excellent, and **Andrew quite** agreed with her. But anticipations of the wonderful change in **his** life, which the letter proposed, possessed and agitated him, and he could think and **talk of nothing** else.

CHAPTER II.

THAT very evening he answered the letter
in terms suggested by his relatives, informing
his " dear uncle " (so he addressed him) of his
mother's death, and accepting the invitation for
himself, provided the old gentleman should
still wish to see him.

"That will give him a chance to write again
and send you money for the journey," said his
sister.

" And show you how much he is in earnest,"
added the brother-in-law.

"He's in earnest, fast enough!" said Andrew. "And I don't see why I should wait
for him to send me money; I've got enough to
get there with, I should think. He says we
are not to expect him to write again."

" But he may change his mind when he hears
that she is dead," suggested Laura.

16

"I don't see why he should," Andrew replied, the bare possibility of the old man's retracting his generous offer casting a chill upon his hopes.

"If he does," she added, "you'll wish you had accepted his invitation before he had a chance to take it back."

"That's so," said her husband, in whose brain, also, the idea of a change of fortune was beginning to work. "My business doesn't grow much here; I've often thought I could do better in the East."

"If Uncle Nathan is so well off, and so desirous of benefiting mother's family, I don't see the need of any of us working so hard as we do," Laura chimed in. "Our three children are growing up and it's going to be pretty expensive to clothe and educate them."

"A little help from the old man won't come amiss," said her husband, with an approving nod. "Truth is, for some time now, I've been getting a little mite tired of harness-making. The same thing, over and over again, day after day, and all my days!"

"Dan will look out for our interest," said Laura.

"I should think he might; we've looked out for him pretty well!" chuckled her husband.

This reminder of his debt of gratitude for the hospitalities of the house, since his mother's death, jarred on Andrew's feelings. He would have much preferred that his brother-in-law should add to that debt by remaining nobly silent about it. He was sorry to be forced also to remember that he had done much in return for these hospitalities, by giving his help in the harness-shop and about the house.

"I guess from what he writes, that Uncle Nathan Petridge has got enough for all," remarked Laura. "And Dan isn't the kind of boy to grab more than his share."

"If I thought he was," laughed her husband, "I should be for rushing right in and taking our chances along with him."

"Maybe you'd better," replied Andrew, irritated as much by the laugh as the serious meaning behind it. His sister's remark, too, had hurt him. " You don't know how much I may grab," he added, with a darkening look.

"Laws, Dan!" exclaimed George, "I didn't think of making you mad! I was only joking."

"Mad?" cried Andrew. "I'm not mad in the least. But when you speak like that, even in joke, I feel that you don't know me. Do you think I wouldn't be just as anxious that Laura and her children should have their share of Uncle Nathan's property as that I should have my own? and more so!" he exclaimed, with choking emotion.

"Of course," George answered, more calmly, but flushing, as he thrust his toil-stained fingers through his hair. "I think you would. At least, I think you think you would, now. And I hope you won't change your mind, when you sail in ahead of us, and find living in a 'pala-shal resdence' is kind of nice, and are tempted to forget your humble relatives in Ohio."

"Heavens!" said the sensitive Andrew, sti-fling with indignation, as he jumped up from the table where he had been writing, and began to walk the floor.

"Now, Dan! George!" exclaimed Laura, distressed, and yet inclined to laugh. "How ridiculous! beginning to quarrel about the old man's property before " —

"I'm not quarrelling," said George.

"Neither am I," said Andrew. "But nobody likes to be twitted unjustly." He stalked to the entry and took down his hat.

"Are you going out, Dan?" called his sister.

"Yes, I am going to mail my letter."

"I'm sorry you vexed him!" said Laura, after he had gone.

"So am I; and I didn't mean to," replied George. "But don't you see? If he steps in before us, he can have it all his own way with old Nate Petridge's property, and leave us out in the cold, if he takes a notion. I 'most wish we were going too!"

Andrew went straight to the post-office, where he dropped his letter, in order that it might leave by the first eastward-bound mail in the morning; then walked the starlit village streets, to cool off his excitement.

Never before had anything like hard words

passed between him and his brother-in-law. He could not forget the sting of them, which was followed, as is often the way with stings, by a swelling and aching more painful than the first injury.

"As if I might defraud them of their rights!" he said to himself, while his feet rustled along the path, for it was now late in September, and the leaves were beginning to fall. "It seems even she thought of that — my own sister! And he had already hinted at the vast amount they have done for me!"

He was more grieved than angry at the recollection; he could forgive the words, but he could never again feel himself a welcome inmate of his brother-in-law's house.

On the other hand, the inducements old Nathan Petridge's letter held out became more and more attractive. Andrew saw himself greeted by a lonely old man in a house which must be to some extent magnificent, if not truly palatial; and imagined, among other luxuries, that of magnanimously securing for his sister's family their full share of the Petridge estate.

He thought of these things until he burned
with impatience to be off, and it seemed no
longer possible for him to wait for another
letter.   Why, indeed, should he wait?

"I'll start to-morrow!" he suddenly exclaimed, as he turned and walked back to his
brother-in-law's house.

CHAPTER III.

LAURA and her husband were not sorry, on the whole, to hear of Andrew's determination, when he announced it to them the next morning. They were almost as eager as he was to learn something definite about the wealth to be inherited; although, to be consistent, George repeated his original advice, that Dan should make sure of what he was to gain, before risking the journey. He also wished to be able to say afterwards, in case the adventure should not turn out well, "It wouldn't have happened, if you had only heard to me!"

Andrew made hasty preparations for the momentous change in his life, putting on his best suit, and taking with him only such clothing as could be packed in a little red valise that had been his father's. Laura and George agreed with him that, if he was going to roll in

23

wealth, he might as well leave his old suits
behind.

He took leave of them in brotherly fashion;
the slight misunderstanding of the evening
before having been put out of memory by the
momentous event of his departure. George
entertained for him a genuine liking and good-
will, and, not simply because he deemed it
especially important to keep on the right side
of him now, he offered to lend him money.

But Andrew felt sure he had enough for the
journey, and did not anticipate needing more
at the end of it. Then Laura came forward
with something which she put into his hand as
he stood holding his valise at the door.

" A letter she wrote to you only a few days
before she died. She said you would soon be
going out into the world, and I was to give it
to you then."

It was carefully sealed. Andrew glanced at
the back of it, and read, in his mother's well-
known handwriting : —

" *To my dear son Andrew, my last written
words, to be read and pondered after I am gone.*"

His face flushed, his lips quivered, and thrusting the letter into his pocket, he turned hurriedly
away; his brother-in-law, who had left his work
to see him off, following and offering to carry
his valise to the train.

Andrew made the journey to Boston without
mishap. There, notwithstanding the bewilder-
ment of finding himself alone in a great,
strange city, he learned, by diligent inquiry,
aided by careful reference to the address given
in Nathan Petridge's letter, that the old man
could probably be reached by one of the horse-
car routes, a few miles out of town.

He got into a car, and watched the sights by
the way with as much interest as his anxiety
regarding the result of his adventure would
permit. He had thought of it with many misgivings since he left his Ohio home, and his
bosom swelled with intensified doubts and
hopes as he neared the end of his trip. A half-
hour's ride brought him to the street which
the conductor told him to take, and he stepped,
with his little red valise, from the platform of
the car.

CHAPTER IV.

No doubt if old Nathan had known of his
coming, he would have had a carriage waiting
for him there. As it was, Andrew wondered
whether or not he ought to take a hack, in
order to reach so fine a house in fitting style;
but no hack was in sight, and after staring
around him for a few moments, he started to
walk up the street.

"Keep right on up the hill; you can't miss
it," said a man gathering pears in a garden,
of whom Andrew made inquiries. "It's pretty
conspicuous."

It was a quiet street, with pleasant resi-
dences not too near together. These, however,
as he advanced, grew more scattered, and the
grounds about them at last gave place to open
fields.

Near the summit of the hill he paused again to look about him. Behind him stretched what seemed an almost interminable village, from the foot of the acclivity, huddling to a city on one side, which, he said to himself, must be Cambridge, and on the other extending, with broken intervals, to a more distant and still greater city, rising to a dome-crowned hill, which he knew was Boston.

Then there was gleaming water in the landscape, flying trains trailing their vaporous flags, here and there trees in their autumnal tints in the foreground, and blue hills rising, still and beautiful and villa-crowned, in the distance. A hazy curtain of smoke and mist hung over all, warmed by an afternoon sun.

Andrew was enraptured by the sight, so different from anything he had ever seen, and he exclaimed aloud: "What a splendid view! What a fine situation for a rich man's residence!"

He was thinking of his uncle's palatial house, which he had expected to find crowning the crest of the hill. Dwellings, in fact, appeared, clustered along the farther slope, but not one of much magnificence, and he found it necessary once more to make inquiries for the Petridge mansion.

The nearest house was a little back from the street, which ran through a deep cut across the summit of the hill. This cut had left the lot on which stood the house, high and desolate, with the front fence undermined here and there by the caving earth, and threatening to tumble down into the highway.

Easy approach to it had been cut off by the grading, but Andrew noticed a rough footpath worn in the face of the bank, and scrambled up by it to the ruined fence.

Stooping under the rail, the palings from which had been removed, he found himself in an extensive dooryard, overgrown with grass and weeds. In the rear stood a little old house, with pigweeds growing to the very door. There was no path leading to it, and the place seemed so wholly uninhabited that Andrew turned away, thinking it useless to pursue his inquiries there.

But instead of descending the bank by the path, he passed on to a large circular space where the grass and weeds were well trodden around a solitary towering chestnut tree. Burrs and leaves, with clubs and stones, and other missiles, covered the ground, and a little way off a dilapidated dry-goods box, which had evidently at one time served as a coal-bin, stood on end.

This was, in fact, a sort of sentry-box; the opening of which being on the farther side, Andrew did not notice a skinny little old man crouching within, grasping a thick cane, and grimacing with malice as he peeped through a crack in the upturned bottom of the box.

Passing along, valise in hand, Andrew kicked the leaves and burrs under his feet, and picked up a chestnut. He cracked it in his teeth, and suddenly remembered that he was hungry. He next took up one of the clubs, that had probably done like service for more than one adventurous boy, and sent it on an errand to the top of the tree.

It went crashing into a thick bough, on the

outer edge of which the brown nuts could be seen clinging in clusters to the open burrs, and brought a number rattling and thumping to the ground.

But as Andrew advanced with a quick step to pick them up, the little old man rushed out of his box, screaming and brandishing his cane.

"I've got ye this time! Surrender! surrender!" and the little old man seized him by the collar with one claw-like hand, while the other still poised the menacing staff.

"What am I to surrender for?" asked the astonished boy.

"For trespassing on my land! For stealing chestnuts!" screamed the little old man.

CHAPTER V.

ANDREW was quite as much amazed as frightened by the apparition of his strange assailant
dashing out and capturing him in that abrupt
fashion. He dodged the cane, which was
shaken unpleasantly near his nose, and grasped
the wrist of the hand that held his collar.

"Why don't you try to get away?" said the
little old man, in an angry, high-pitched voice.
"Why didn't you run away like all the rest of
'em?"

"I saw no reason for running," Andrew
replied, looking down on his captor with wondering, candid eyes. "I didn't know they were
your chestnuts."

"You knew they were somebody's!" panted
the little old man, with failing voice and
breath, while he trembled from head to foot
with excitement.

31

"I suppose they are somebody's," Andrew
replied, "and if I had known anybody lived
here, I wouldn't have touched 'em.   Why
don't you have a sign — No TRESPASSING?"

"That's just what I have, but the boys pull
it off from the tree and fling it away, and then
come for chestnuts, and pretend they don't
know they are trespassing.   I never could
catch one before, they run so."

"Well, you've caught me.   What are you
going to do with me?" Andrew inquired.

"That's just it!" replied the little old man.
His hand shook so that it had fairly shaken
itself off the boy's collar, and so far from
brandishing his cane, he was now leaning on
it for support. "I don't know what to do with
a boy that don't run, nor try to get away."

"I'll tell you what you'd better do," said
Andrew.

"What's that?" said the little old man.

"Let me go," said Andrew.

"Give me something!   Pay ransom!" said
the little old man, with gleaming eyes.

"How much?" Andrew asked.

"A hundred dollars!" ejaculated the little old man.

"That seems an enormous ransom," said Andrew. "If I was a prince or a millionaire — but I haven't a tenth part of a hundred dollars in the world!"

"Your relatives have!" retorted the little old man. "Come, they'll pay that and more, rather than see you go to jail."

"Go to jail?" Andrew gave his captor a dry, discouraging smile. Though barely seventeen, he was almost head and shoulders taller than his captor, who seemed a mere squeaking pigmy beside him.

"Yes, I'll drag you there!"

"You'll drag me?" Andrew spoke with a good-natured drawl, and grinned down at the little old man. "I'm afraid you'd find it pretty hard dragging."

"Give me twenty-five cents!" cried the eager little old man.

There was something so ludicrous in this sudden collapse in his demand for ransom, that Andrew, though harrassed and vexed, and anxious to be on his way, was obliged to laugh.

"No, I won't give even that — I might be cheating you. I have only one relative who has money, and I am on my way to his house now. I'll lay the case before him, and what he says you ought to have, you shall have."

"Who is he?" demanded the little old man.

"Nathan Petridge," replied Andrew. "I came in here to inquire for his house; that's what brought me inside your fence — if you call that a fence."

"Nathan Petridge!" squeaked the little old man.

"Yes; why not? You may not believe it, but Nathan Petridge — you must know him, for he lives somewhere on this hill — is my uncle. Or, if not exactly my uncle "—

"Nathan Petridge!" again gasped the little old man. "I'm Nathan Petridge myself!"

CHAPTER VI.

ANDREW turned pale with momentary astonished incredulity.

"And who are you?" cried the little old man.

"I don't know! I don't know anything! I thought — where do you live?" Andrew asked, recovering from his stupor, and trying to think the *dénouement* of his romance might not be so bad as it appeared.

"I live here," said Nathan Petridge, pointing with his heavy cane to the house behind the pigweeds.

"That is your palatial residence!" said Andrew, looking over the old man's head with a strange, glassy, despairing smile. "Well," after a pause, with trembling lips and in a husky voice, "then I don't see anything left for me to do but to turn around and go back to Ohio!"

But all at once the thought occurred to him that he had no money to go back with.

"To Ohio!" echoed Nathan Petridge. "You come from Ohio?"

"All the way from Ohio, in answer to your letter to my mother!" said Andrew, burning with wrath and mortification, as he began to realize what his folly had led to. "What did you mean by writing such a letter as that?"

"I've written no letter! I never write letters!" Nathan Petridge replied.

"Then somebody has written in your name," said Andrew. "Look here!" taking the letter from his pocket. "Do you know anything about this?"

"Yes, yes! that's what I wrote to Jane Hapnell, she that was a Boynton! And it's true. There's room for all."

"Where?" Andrew demanded.

"In my house," said the old man, with ridiculous conceit. "I've more of a house than you think. Come in! Come in! Welcome to the Petridge mansion!"

He was bareheaded, his hat having fallen off

when he rushed out of his sentry-box. He
wore no linen, and in place of a cravat an inde-
scribable old rag was twisted about his shrivelled neck. He had a thin beard, which showed
his unwholesome skin under it; and he was
sallow and wrinkled as a dried pea. His grimacing smile, and bows and flourishes of exces-
sive politeness, astonished the ungainly lad who
stood staring at him, even more than his pre-
vious rude onset.

"So, Jane Hapnell is your mother? Jane
Boynton that was!" The old man turned to
pick up his hat, which he set on the head of
his stout cane instead of his own bald pate.
"Jabez Boynton was her father — a good friend
of mine; he gave me my start in life. But
come! no more ceremony! once for all!"

Thereupon he caused his cane, with the hat
upon it, to bow low before his visitor, as he
backed away toward the house. Andrew would
hardly have understood that this was to be
regarded as an act of courtesy, had not the old
man, as he walked on before him, frequently
turned and made the hatted staff do the bow-

ing, very fantastically, while he repeated his
hospitable invitations.

It was a much-battered and shapeless hat ;
quite in keeping with the old man's tattered
clothing and shoes trodden down at the heel.
Andrew followed wonderingly, half-inclined to
laugh, and half to cry with disappointment and
heaviness of heart.

"I may as well stop and see how he lives,
anyway," he said to himself; "and whether he's
crazy or a fool."

" Tarry here," said the old man, having led
the way through the pigweeds to the front
door, " while I go around and unlock from the
inside. We usually," he added, " reserve this
entrance for state occasions." And with a final
ceremonious bow from the hat and cane, he
disappeared around the corner of the house.

Andrew stood holding his little red valise,
and winking hard as if to make himself realize
where he was and what was happening, when
presently was heard the sound of feet clatter-
ing along a bare floor within, followed by the
grating of a rusty lock or bolt. Then the bow-

ing hat reappeared in the open door, with the smiling old man behind it.

"It's the plague of servants," said **Nathan**, apologetically, " that they **are** never on hand when wanted. I maintain three, and **have** to wait on myself. This is the vestibule," he ex-plained, showing the boy into a barren **entry**; "and here is my suite **of** apartments."

Andrew found himself **in a** room **of good** size, but dingy and desolate. **The windows** were cobwebbed **and** curtainless; and paper-hangings of **a** very old and faded pattern, with roses as big **as** cabbages, covered the **walls in** streaks and spots **only,** leaving much **of** the smoky and grimy plastering exposed.

There was a tumbled bed in **one** corner, a small cooking-stove in another, and a rickety pine table **on one** side, besides two decrepit chairs, with worn splint bottoms, mended by crossed and knotted cords.

"Will you enter the library or the drawing-room ?" said old Nathan, ushering the lad along with his bowing cane. " Everything, as you see, is **on** a magnificent scale, and an en-tirely new plan."

He proudly pointed at the floor, which was curiously portioned off into rectangular spaces by lengths of coarse twine stretched across.

"There, you see, is the culinary department, in other words, kitchen, which you will always know by the stove being in it. The dining-room is adjoining, indicated by the table. Now we are in the library, and now" — he hopped over one of the lengths of string — " I am in the drawing-room. See how ingenious and very convenient it is!"

He stood eyeing his visitor with a pleased and triumphant simplicity, which puzzled and astonished him more and more.

"Here! set your valise in the library," the old man went on. " I regret the absence of my servants: Benjamin, the butler and bottle-washer; Thomas, the chief cook and steward, and Susan and Mary, the maids," — Andrew noticed that his three servants had grown to four, — " all gallivanting somewhere, just as distinguished company has arrived. Have you had supper?"

"Nothing but a couple of chestnuts, which

didn't agree with me," Andrew answered dryly.
He had no thought of prolonging his visit to the
old man an hour; yet he sank down mechanically in one of the mended splint-bottomed
chairs.

"Lobster salad, veal cutlet, chicken fricassee, — which shall it be?" old Nathan asked,
with smiling hospitality. "Speak the word."

To see what he would do, Andrew answered:
"If it's all one to you, I'll say chicken fricassee."

"Chicken fricassee!" repeated the old man,
his smile becoming thoughtful. "I declare, I
believe that rascally steward has gone off and
left the larder empty. And I'm afraid you'd
find it irksome waiting for him to return and
cook your supper. But I'm bound to entertain
you while you are here. Will you do me a
favor?"

Without waiting for a reply, he thrust a hand
into his pocket, and went on:

"Go to the bakeshop on the corner of the
next street below, and buy a five-cent loaf of
bread; and to the grocery opposite and invest

for me two cents in smoked herrings. And, in honor of your arrival, three cents for a pint of milk. Or don't you care for milk? I guess we can dispense with the milk," he added, as he counted out some pennies on the table. "Seven cents will do as well as ten. A penny saved is a penny earned!" And with a shrewd smile he dropped the change which remained in his hand back into his pocket.

"In your letter, you boast of your millions," Andrew could not forbear reminding him.

"But I don't carry millions in my breeches pockets," the old man answered, shrewdly. "I may have herds of cattle and yet be bothered if you ask me for a beefsteak. I have wealth! I have wealth!" he added, gleefully. "But I am beset by robbers, and have to be careful. That's why I sent for Sister Jane and her family."

"I don't see what we can do for you," Andrew answered, stern and gloomy, in his chagrin and indignation.

"You don't see? I'll tell you!" Old Nathan sat down in the drawing-room and talked with

Andrew in the library, over the dividing string.
He set his cane on the floor and leaned forward
upon it.

"I have relatives that are trying, by fair
means or foul, generally foul, to possess them-
selves of my property. But I am too much
for them!" and the old man showed his gums
and three or four scattered stubs of front teeth
with a grotesque grin. "I'll tell you about
it."

Andrew was intending, every moment, to
leave that wretched place and that strange old
man; yet he stayed on.

The sun had by this time gone down, and
the room, its scanty furniture, the plastered
walls with their still adhering patches of paper,
the floor with its whimsical twine partitions,
and the old man leaning forward on his cane,
all took on the gloom of the sudden twilight,
while a deeper gloom fell upon the spirit of the
bewildered boy.

CHAPTER VII.

THE old man in the parlor hitched his chair
a little nearer Andrew in the library, showing
a proper respect for the string partition, which
he was careful never to put his foot upon, and
proceeded to explain, —

"My own blood relations! Solomon Burge
and his family. Solomon Burge is my nephew,
my own sister's son. He got himself appointed
my guardian on the ground that I was insane!
Did you ever hear anything like it?" cried
Nathan. "Do I show the slightest symptoms
of unsoundness here?" tapping his forehead.

As Andrew made no answer, he went on, —

"They even clapped me into a hospital; but
they couldn't lay hands on my money, after all.
I'd put that where they couldn't find it; and
as they had my expenses to pay, they was glad

44

to take me out again; they dropped me like a
hot potater! Now what I want is somebody to
stand between me and them. So I thought of
Jane. And how is she? I believe it is thirty
year since I've seen Sister Jane, she that was
a Boynton."

"Then you haven't received my letter,
written the night before I started?" said
Andrew.

"I've received no letter; I never receive
letters," answered the old man.

Andrew hardly thought it worth while to
explain to him that his mother was dead.
With a heavy heart, miserably irresolute, he
took up his valise and rose to depart.

"Here's the money; don't go without the
money," said the old man, adding further
directions for finding the bakehouse.

"I'm not going for the bread; I don't care
for any supper," said Andrew.

"Don't care for supper?" cried the old man,
with a hopeful gleam. "Then one smoked
herring will answer." He dropped another of
the pennies back into his ragged trousers.

"But you may get the loaf; we shall want breakfast."

With a wretchedly hollow feeling at heart, Andrew was moving toward the door, when he suddenly changed his mind. "I'll get the loaf and the smoked herring for *you*," he said, thinking the errands would afford him an opportunity to make inquiries regarding the old man.

"You'll leave your valise?" cried Nathan, hesitating before putting the money into his hand. Andrew smiled drearily, and to show that he had no intention of running away with the loaf and smoked herring, he yielded the valise.

He went out through an empty shed in the rear of the house, and found himself again on the open hill-top. This proved to be a dome-like crest of a few acres, surrounded by steep sides, where it was in process of cutting down to a much lower grade to make room for village streets, an innovation which, it was evident, would soon undermine the Petridge house itself, and sweep it into oblivion. It stood there, as it were on an island, under the crumbling cliffs of which the sea of a more modern civilization was fast encroaching, and it was probably this fate awaiting it which had caused it to be left in its neglected condition, in the possession of so strange an occupant.

It was a relief to Andrew to breathe once more the outer air. A delicious coolness had fallen upon the earth. The fragrance peculiar to autumn evenings floated up with the mist from the valley. A tranquil sunset flamed in the western sky.

He scrambled down the caving bank, in the direction of a populous part of the town behind the hill, and found his way to the bakehouse. He looked in, hoping to see a man with whom he could have some talk about Mr. Petridge. Finding only a young girl, and being a bashful boy, he would have gone away again if he had not remembered the loaf he had come for.

The girl was lighting a kerosene lamp at a desk behind a row of glass cases containing a tempting array of cakes and tarts and pies.

By the glow it shed upon her brow and hair, he saw that she had a round, fresh face, with large, laughing eyes, and a charming little turned-up nose. He hardly knew whether the lamp or her pleasant features gave the more light. If not exactly smiling, they seemed ever on the point of breaking into a smile.

The smile came when he advanced to the counter, and, resting his closed hand on the glass case, asked for a five-cent loaf. He was lank and shy; he spoke with a peculiar drawl; it was plain enough that he was a stranger in the place. The loaf was produced and wrapped in brown paper, and the closed hand dropped its rattling pennies on the glass case.

"Anything else?" she said, her pretty inflection and her pert nose turning up at him with frank good-nature.

"It is for Mr. Petridge," he said, as he hesitatingly drew his purchase toward him.

"Is he sick again?" she asked. "I haven't seen him for a week."

Andrew was ready to pour out his troubles to any one who would listen to him. He stood leaning awkwardly against the counter, his eyes were downcast upon his loaf, and there was a convulsive movement in his throat before he spoke. She had a laughing nature, ever ready to ripple over at the slightest provocation, but the sight of his emotion sobered her.

"I don't know whether he is sick," he replied, "but something is the matter with him. What is it?"

"Oh, he's crazy!" she said. "Not very bad. He harms nobody."

"He has harmed me!" said Andrew, out of the fulness of his heart. "I've come all the way from Ohio on his invitation. He wrote that he was rich, and living in style."

"That's his hobby," the girl replied. She kept a serious countenance, in view of his distress, but now and then her habitual laugh would flash out like summer lightning in an evening sky. Andrew forgot his diffidence; he stood holding the loaf under his arm, and turned his honest, earnest eyes full upon her.

"Has he really any property?" he asked.

"That's a mystery," she replied. "Some think he is a miser, and has heaps of money. He manages somehow to buy his bread and cheese."

"I don't know what to think," said Andrew, sorely perplexed. He told more of his unhappy story, and asked, "Is there a place near here where I can get supper and lodging, not very expensive?"

She was directing him to a restaurant, when a stoutish woman, with a full, florid, amiable face, entered from a passage beyond the desk, bringing a broad tray of hot rolls in her plump arms.

"Ma, just think!" exclaimed the girl. "Mr. Petridge wrote to this young man's folks in the West, pretending to be awfully rich, and offering them a home; and he has come hundreds of miles to see him, and now he don't know what to do!"

The woman questioned him with motherly interest, and exclaimed: "He's as miserable a human being as I know anywhere! The idea of *his* taking care of his connections! What he

needs is somebody to take care of *him*. If any
of his friends had come from the West with
that purpose, I should be thankful."

"Don't his relatives here do anything for
him?" asked Andrew.

"About all they do is to plague and pester
him, in the notion that he has money, which
they're afraid he'll lose or give away."

ANDREW IN THE BAKERSHOP.

CHAPTER VIII.

YEARNING for advice and comfort, Andrew
would have been glad to talk further with the
friendly mother and daughter, but they were
obliged to attend to other customers coming
in. They seemed quite to forget his presence;
the girl was laughing and chatting as if there
were no such wretch in existence, and he went
off, with his misery and his loaf.

He was ashamed to buy only one herring at
the grocer's, so he called for half-a-dozen, using
some of his own money to complete the purchase. Then he hurried back to the old house
on the hill.

Harassed in mind as he was, he couldn't
help stopping to wonder at the scene which met
his gaze from the top. The cities and towns
he had beheld before were now more dimly

52

outlined in the evening mists and shades, but everywhere shone lights in homes and streets, thick as stars in the sky; some near, some far and faint, some hazily reflected in water, like rows of lamps on a bridge. At the same time, the dull, distant, muffled roar of life came to him, wafted on the cool, damp air. What a vast, busy, lonely, preoccupied, tumultuous world it was to the soul of the solitary boy!

His future was darker than the night, but the first step to be taken was clear in his mind; to give the old man his loaf and his herrings, take instant leave of him, and seek his own supper and lodging elsewhere.

Approaching the door with this determination, he heard appalling sounds within. All was dark, and, in his fright, Andrew was on the point of dropping his bundles and running away.

But the sounds were undoubtedly human groans, and his conscience would not let him run. He paused under the empty shed, lifted the latch of the house door noiselessly, listened a moment longer, thrilled to the soul by a

louder groan than the rest, then resolutely
went in.

The sounds proceeded from the corner of
the room where the bed was, and there, in the
deep gloom, Andrew found the old man con-
vulsed with pain, his hands clenched and his
knees drawn up.

"What is the matter?" he asked, bending
anxiously over him.

"One of my spasms," replied the old man,
between his groans. "The worst I ever had!
It will kill me this time."

"What — how — where is the pain?" Andrew had by this time forgotten his own fears,
in his terrified sympathy for the old man.

"They told me at the hospital it was the
stomach, but it's the heart! I know it's the
heart! Don't take that!"

Andrew was about to remove some object
which seemed to be in the way of the sufferer's
convulsive writhing, for he was constantly hit-
ting it. It proved to be the old man's cane,
which lay beside him on the bed.

"Let me set it in the corner," said Andrew.

"No, no, leave it be!" The old man clutched it wildly with both hands. "It's my only defence against *them!*"

"Who?" said Andrew.

"Robbers! My relations! Them that would tear my heart out to get my money. If I die — boy, boy, hear me!"

One bony hand released its hold of the cane, in order to clutch Andrew's arm.

"Hear my last words! If I die, don't let them touch a penny of it! not a penny!"

"How can I help it? I don't know where your money is."

"I'll tell you!" said the old man. "Put down your head; even the walls have ears. Promise that you will be faithful; not to leave me till I'm" —

Here his difficult utterance ended in another wild spasm.

"What can I do for you?" asked Andrew.

"Nothing. The fit has to take its course. Another such wrench will end me. Ah, and I haven't told you!"

"Tell me," said Andrew, putting down his ear so as not to lose a word.

"I've been a lifetime saving it up, and now if it should fall into their hands, I couldn't sleep in my grave. It shall all be yours, every cent; only stay by me! Don't forsake a dying old man!"

"I won't leave you." Nathan Petridge now lay stretched out upon the bed, breathing heavily, but free from his agonizing cramps. "I'm waiting to hear you," Andrew added, with intense curiosity.

"Ah, yes; you shall know before I die., But as death seemed to have relaxed his grip for a time, the old man clung to his precious secret. "So you are really the son of Sister Jane? You shall have it, in trust for her, every dollar! Only promise again! Don't leave me to die alone!"

"Certainly I will not! There must be something I can do. Let me strike a light."

"Yes, yes! There's matches in the oyster-shell on the mantelpiece."

Andrew found them, struck one, and lit a kerosene lamp which stood on the table. He turned, and by the dim light looked at the pitiful figure, now drawn up in a heap, on the tossed bed.

" You need some nourishing food, some warm drink," he said.

" It is too late," replied Nathan. " I've had nothing but chestnuts and a couple of apples for three days. If I had only biled 'em ! And then the excitement of meeting you ! Your hands ! "

Andrew sat down on the bed, and gave the old man his hands, which he held quietly for a few minutes, and then wrung spasmodically through another convulsion.

" Let me call a doctor, won't you ? " said Andrew.

" No, no ! doctors charge like thunder, and their medicines are pizen. Turn down the lamp a little ; no need of burning so much oil. "

Andrew was glad of an occasion to withdraw his hands from the old man's clutch. But hardly had he reduced the flame of the lamp sufficiently, when the sick man called him back to the bedside.

" You are Sister Jane's own boy; I will make

your fortune and hers. Don't leave me an instant, but watch me closely, and let me know if I am going to die, so I can tell you " —

His voice became inaudible, his limbs relaxed, his eyes closed ; and it was in vain that Andrew, who thought he might be dying, exhorted him to tell his secret. His breathing became more regular, his hard, dry features grew moist, and his tight hold of the boy gradually loosened. The old man was asleep.

CHAPTER IX.

ANDREW withdrew his hands, with a sigh of
relief; he took his eyes from the sickly, aged,
emaciated face, and glanced about the dismal
room, trying to realize his extraordinary situation. He hardly dared move; it seemed terrible for him to remain in that awful silence,
broken only by the sleeper's heavy breathing,
and yet he could not go away.

Who would have believed that he would
remain an hour in that house, after learning
how shamefully he had been deluded? And
yet here he was, a night-watcher by the bedside of a miserable, sick, and insane old man.

Doubts and questions crowded upon his excited brain. It seemed to him that Mr. Petridge must have a hidden hoard somewhere;
but when he glanced down at the floor, with
its ridiculous string partitions, in strange con-

trast with the reality of pain and misery there present, the old man's boasted riches appeared as phantasmal as the palatial residence to which Sister Jane and her family had been invited.

"I wish he would wake up, so I can go and get my supper," thought Andrew. "I wonder if I ought to break my promise and leave him?"

He was faint with hunger; for the truth was, he had not only had no supper, but his dinner had been postponed in anticipation of the entertainment awaiting him at the Petridge mansion. He looked askance at the package of smoked herrings, and the white loaf bursting out of its brown wrapper, where he had placed them on the table. Presently he reached for the bread and broke off a piece, which he munched with relish, enlivened by the flavor of one of the herrings.

A good part of the loaf and four of the herrings went to allay the cravings of the healthy boy's appetite; and he regretted that he had not also bought the milk the old man at first so generously proposed. He remembered see-

ing a pump in the rear of the house, the thought
of which preyed upon him, and made him so
thirsty that he finally got up on tiptoe, and
started in search of water. He found a broken-
nosed pitcher on a pantry shelf, and starting
out of the back door with it, he tried the pump.
A few strokes brought the cold water from the
well splashing upon the wooden platform; he
filled the broken-nosed pitcher, and lifted it
dripping to his lips.

He drank, and then holding the pitcher in
both hands, paused to look about him and think.
Never afterward could he forget that moment
at the well. A thousand lights twinkled; over
Boston hung an immense luminous haze, and
farther to the east beamed a more effulgent
glory. It was the rising moon, swelling up red
and huge from the horizon, — Andrew did not
know that the sea was there, — and shooting
its watery beams through fog-drifts and city-
smokes, over innumerable roofs, to the spot
where he stood. It touched the old pump on
its rotting platform; a dilapidated trellis pro-
jecting half-way over it, like a ruined arbor,

from the shed at the end of the house; and the house itself, so gloomy and silent, with its strange inmate.

" How odd that I am here!" Andrew thought; and his mind went back with lightning speed to the afternoon when he had left his Ohio home, and his sister had put a certain letter into his hand.

The rumor of his going East, to take advantage of a great fortune offered him, had spread quickly through the village, and a troop of young friends had come to the railroad station to see him off. He remembered how proudly conscious he was of being admired and envied by them then; how they had begged him to write to them, as if it would be a great conde-scension on his part, and waved their hats and handkerchiefs to him looking back, as he rode away on the platform of his car.

How would he be regarded by those envious admirers if he should return to them now? He imagined their derisive greetings; and he could hear his kind but blunt-speaking brother-in-law's exasperating "I told you so!" But out of all

these images rose one more distinct than the
rest ; his mother's letter.

He had read it more than once, and not without emotion, after getting away from familiar
scenes and faces, on the flying railroad train ;
but his mind had been too full of anticipations
of a brilliant future, to take in all its tender and
deep significance. Amidst his ruined hopes, in
the solitude of that night on the hill, in the
rays of the red moon, the desire rose within him
to read again those last words written by the
dying hand.

He went back softly into the house. The
old man lay quiet, but muttering in his sleep.
The room was filled with a disagreeable odor
from the lamp, which Andrew had hardly per-
ceived before going out into the fresh evening
air. He turned up the sulking light into a
more cheerful flame, and taking the letter from
his breast pocket, sat down with it by the
table.

He unfolded it now with far different sensa-
tions from those with which he had first opened
it. Then it was full of the sacred, almost too-

painful memories of the past. It was now a comforter and counsellor in time of trouble.

His eyes, as he read, were more than once blinded by unshed tears, before he came to these words : —

" O my son, I pray you always to remember that an upright, manly character is to be prized above honors and riches. When I think of this I am reconciled to what would otherwise be a grief to me, that I shall leave you a poor boy, with your living to earn by hard work. That work, if you accept it cheerfully, will be better for you than wealth. I should dread to know that you were to come into possession of great riches.

" I trust you will achieve a competence, but do not be anxious about it, and, O my son, do not try to acquire it in haste. Be contented to get on slowly in paths of patient industry, enjoying each day, helping others, doing always the present duty, and biding your time.

" Take that as your watchword. Accept no pleasure nor advantage before it is rightfully yours. In hours of grief and trial, do not lose

"AGAIN AND AGAIN THE BOY READ THOSE WORDS." Page 65.

heart. All doubt, all evil will pass away, and all good things come round to you in due season, if you are brave and faithful, and bide your time."

Again and again the boy read those words, and sat and pondered them, with his hands fallen with the letter upon his knees, and his eyes looking far beyond the dingy walls of that lonely room, into the world of thoughts those feebly traced lines called up.

"I'll do it!" he said, at last, with fervent lips, "I'll do my duty, if I can find out what it is, and bide my time."

CHAPTER X.

HOW IT CHANCED THAT THE BAKER'S WIFE CARRIED A
BROTH TO THE OLD MISER.

ADJOINING the bakery were the living rooms
of the house; there the baker's family were
at their cosey breakfast the next morning,
when a servant, left in charge of the shop,
announced, —

"A lanky young chap wants to see 'the
woman.' I guess he must mean you, Mrs.
Wilbur."

"It's that ridiculous tall boy from Ohio!"
exclaimed Phronie, the daughter, with fun and
sympathy flashing up in her vivacious face.
"I must go with you, ma; he's as good as a
play."

The "ridiculous tall boy" it was indeed,
looking haggard and worn, as he stood with his
hands in his pockets gazing down at the pies
and cakes in the glass cases. Mrs. Wilbur

66

scrutinized him keenly, and asked how he got
on with the old man.

"I'm afraid he's pretty sick," said Andrew.
"He had several dying spells in the night.
He pulled through and slept, but he's so weak
this morning he can't get up. He won't have
a doctor, and I don't know what to do. I
thought maybe you could tell me."

"Pretty rough on you, my boy!" said the
baker's wife.

"There wasn't so much fun in it as there
might be. I've passed better nights," Andrew
said, with so dry a drawl and with so solemn a
countenance that Phronie, watching him from
behind the counter, with eyes full of pathetic
interest, burst into a giggle.

Mrs. Wilbur gave her a chiding look, and
asked, turning to Andrew, "What are you
going to do?"

"That's what I'd like to know," he replied.
"I can't leave him, and I don't see how I can
stay. An old man and his cudgel aren't the
best company in the world. He even sleeps
with his club, for fear of robbers. I believe

he's starved.   He needs something to eat
besides baker's bread and smoked herrings.
No disrespect to your bread!" he hastened to
add.

"I know what he wants!" exclaimed the
baker's wife. "It isn't the best baker's bread
in or about Boston, which may be ours or some
other shop's; that's neither here nor there.
It's a good, warm, nourishing broth, and that
he shall have, if I turn to and make it myself."

"If you will," said Andrew, gratefully, "I
will pay you for it."

"I don't want your pay!" she replied, fret-
fully. "If anybody pays for it, it shall be the
old miser. It puts me out of all manner of
patience to see a human creature treat himself
as he does!"

Andrew made his own breakfast of hot rolls
and a piece of Washington pie, while the broth
was preparing. He walked about as he ate,
thinking intently, but having no unnecessary
conversation with the girl, whose tittering had
wounded his pride. He couldn't help looking
at her now and then, however, and almost

every time he did so, he caught her watching
him with large, bright, wistful, sympathizing
eyes.

The baker's wife brought out the broth in a
quart pail from the living part of the house,
and Andrew noticed that she had on her bonnet and shawl.

"I guess I'd better go up with you," she
said, "and see if anything else can be done for
Mr. Petridge." She was glad of an excuse to
look in and see how the old man lived; she
had heard so much about his oddities, his miser-
liness, and the string partitions on his floor.
But she had a worthier motive at heart.

"It's heathenish to leave neighbors to suffer
and die alone, no matter who or what they are."

As Andrew went out with her, Phronie's
eyes still followed him, looking as if she would
like to go too.

"What a place to climb!" said the baker's
wife, as Andrew helped her up the easiest
ascent of the steep hill-top. "Modern improvement!" she panted, out of breath with
the exertion. "It's a good thing, I suppose,

but it seems a pity to cut away the old fortifications."

"What old fortifications?" Andrew inquired. He had already noticed behind Nathan's lot a curious low, zigzag embankment,
overgrown with grass.

"Those are the old earthworks. They date
back to Revolutionary times and the siege of
Boston," replied the baker's wife. "The
American forces threw them up when they
occupied the height after the battle of Bunker
Hill, or what was called by mistake 'Bunker
Hill.' That isn't far off; where the monument
stands, over in Charlestown."

He had observed the soaring granite shaft,
and wondered what it was. He had read his
country's history with a boy's patriotic fervor,
and this information awakened in him a new
interest.

But now the condition of the old man
required his attention. They found him lying
on his bed, with his clothes on, which he had
lain down in the night before, and with his
cudgel by his side. He made an attempt to

rise, on hearing footsteps and voices enter, but sank down again from exhaustion.

"I beg pardon!" he grimaced. "This is not the way to receive a lady. If my servants were not playing truant! I vow, I'll discharge all five of 'em! Show her into the library, or drawing-room, or" —

"Bother his library and drawing-room and five servants!" muttered the baker's wife, looking about her with a thrifty housekeeper's scowl of amazement. "Have you a bowl for this broth?"

Mr. Petridge ate ravenously, and smacked his shrivelled lips as he lay back on the bed. Then Mrs. Wilbur looked over the house with Andrew. They found a scantily furnished pantry, and, upstairs, a low-roofed attic, with bare boards overhead and rusty shingle-nails sticking through, a chimney at one end, and a window at the other.

The most interesting discovery was a bed under the rafters, with a husk mattress and a bolster.

"Dry as need be," the baker's wife ex-

claimed, thrusting her hand into the tick,
"thanks to the sun on the roof! This will
be just the thing for you, if you stay with him,
and I don't see how he can be left alone, at
least for a day or two. Maybe I can manage
to spare you a pair of sheets and a bed-quilt,
and make you comfortable in other ways. If
you were a girl now, I'd set you to cleaning up
his house a little."

"Perhaps I might do it as it is," said Andrew, not very well pleased with the prospect.

"If possible, I'll let one of my servant girls
come up and help you," Mrs. Wilbur replied,
as they returned to the room below. "You'll
want some cloths to wash windows with; I
wonder if he has anything to make a fire
with?"

"I've burnt a few chestnut-burrs lately,"
piped the old miser from his pillow.

"Chestnut fiddlesticks!" said the baker's
wife. "Is that all the fuel you have?"

"The clubs the boys bring to fling into the
tree. And the fence, the palings on the fence,"
said the old man.

CHAPTER XI.

TELLING Andrew she would have some
things ready for him, if he would come down to
the bakehouse in half an hour, Mrs. Wilbur de-
parted. He then found a battered axe, broke
up some of the fence with it, started a fire, and
put on a kettle of water to warm. This done,
he looked down with a sad grin at the string
partitions; they must come up the first thing.

The old man remonstrated shrilly when,
having found a hammer, Andrew began to pull
the nails out of the floor; but he persisted,
declaring that it was confusing for him to live
in so many rooms at once, and that if the partitions remained, he would have to go. This
brought the old man to terms; the strings were
removed, and the floor swept.

73

So much accomplished, Andrew started to
go for the things Mrs. Wilbur had promised
him. At the top of the path leading down the
caved bank he met a young girl climbing up.
It was Phronie, bringing a scrubbing-brush and
rags. She turned up at him her pert little nose,
and broke into a gay laugh as he helped her up
the bank.

"Ma couldn't spare a girl for an hour or two,
so she said I might come and bring these things,
and show you how to wash windows if you
want to make a start. Won't it be fun?"

Andrew had not regarded it as fun up to this
moment. Although by no means a lazy boy,
he had generally found work in which he was
not specially interested more or less irksome.
For that reason it had been hard for him, since
his mother's death, to settle down to any steady
employment; he was waiting for something he
was sure to like.

But since reading over her letter the night
before, he had resolved to do cheerfully the
first plain duty that came to his hand. That
seemed to be to make old Nathan a little more

decent and comfortable during the short time
he remained with him.

"I don't feel that I owe him anything," he
said, talking with Phronie on their way to the
house; "but I came here willing that he should
take care of me. Then why shouldn't I do
what little I can for him?"

"I think you are very forgiving," Phronie
said, "after his fooling you so."

"I was a fool to be fooled by him," Andrew
replied. "I don't know why I shouldn't forgive him."

She looked up at him archly. "And have
you forgiven me?" The dimples about her
mouth were like the folded petals of a laugh,
just ready to open.

"For what?" Andrew asked; and yet he
knew.

"For tittering at something you said this
morning," she replied, the laugh flashing out.
"It was very wicked in me; but do you
know, you've the funniest way of speaking
sometimes! I suppose it's a kind of Western
drawl."

"It's not a Western drawl; it's *my* drawl," said Andrew. "You may laugh at it. I know I'm a gawky."

"Oh, no, you're not that!" she assured him, suppressing her risibility. "Only a little — I don't know what — queer."

He blushed to the tips of his ears, which, by the way, were large, and stood out from his head like a small pair of wings. He wished for a moment he could make some sharp criticism upon her in return; but his resentment was short-lived.

"Tell me how I'm queer," he said, "and try to improve me. I'm only a green Ohio boy, anyway."

"Do you want to know just what I think?" she cried, with her bright, round, arch, tender, merry face beaming up at him. She was rather short, and her pretty head, with its inverted bird's-nest of a small bonnet (the fashion of the day) came up only to his shoulder.

"Yes, tell me!" he said, holding himself firm, prepared to hear the worst.

"When we get a little better acquainted,"

she replied. "I don't care, though; I'll tell you now. I think you are as honest as the day is long, and as good-hearted as you can be."

There was something besides mere fun in the face that said this. He laughed, too, with relief and pleasure, and said, "That's worth coming all the way from Ohio to hear."

"Didn't anybody ever compliment you before?"

"I guess not. I never was very popular at home till the news got around that I was to be adopted by a millionaire. Then I had popularity enough in one day to last a lifetime." He added, with a rueful smile, "I wonder how popular I shall be if I go back now!"

"But you are not going back!" said Phronie.

"I don't know," he replied, his countenance clouding. "What else can I do? But I mustn't think of that; I shall go as crazy as Uncle Nathan if I do."

"Do you call him *uncle?* I thought he was no relation."

"He isn't. But I was ready enough to call

him *uncle* when I thought he was going to enrich me, and I ought not to be ashamed to do so now. That's my window up there," he said, pointing to the attic. "It has one good thing, a splendid outlook."

"What a lovely hill it is, or used to be!" exclaimed Phronie. "I've often been up here to see the sunsets, or the steam-trains going out in the early morning, on all the roads — oh, it's superb!"

They entered the house, where Andrew brushed down the cobwebs while she dusted the window sashes. She then showed him how the panes were to be cleaned and rubbed, setting the example with her own hands, which she proudly declared were not afraid of work. She had put up her sleeves and pinned back her skirt, and he had taken off his coat.

Having become reconciled to the innovation, old Nathan chuckled with glee to see the work going on. Suddenly she exclaimed, peering through a pane she was rubbing: "There's somebody at the chestnut tree! the Burge boys!"

CHAPTER XII.

THE old man clutched his cane, and started up in great excitement.

"I'll attend to them," said Andrew. "Only give me authority to drive 'em away."

"It's the tribe that's trying to get my money!" cried the old man, reeling back upon the bed. "I'll have 'em prosecuted!"

"Are they really his relatives?" Andrew inquired, as Phronie followed him out through the shed, where he paused to put on his coat.

"Their father is his nephew," she replied, trying to keep him back. "They're a bad lot. Better have nothing to do with 'em."

He stepped forward, rather reluctantly, it must be owned, and passed the corner of the house. Seeing three young fellows, — two of them almost full-grown men — clubbing the chestnut tree, he asked them, with his dry

79

drawl, if they were aware that they were
trespassing.

"What business is it of yours?" said the
youngest of the three, a saucy-faced boy of
fifteen, while the others continued to pick up
the nuts their last clubs had brought down.

"Mr. Petridge has sent me to warn you off,"
replied Andrew.

"And who are you?" cried the second of
the three brothers, caricaturing Andrew's
drawl.

"I'm taking care of him just now," said
Andrew, turning very red. "He says if you
don't leave he'll have you prosecuted."

Thereupon the oldest of the three, stooping
to pick up a chestnut, took up a club instead.
He was tall and athletic, with an insolent face
looking out from under a slouched felt hat.
He did not hurl the club into the tree, but
held it at his side, while he took a menacing
stride toward Andrew.

"I heard of you," he said, with his under
jaw out and canted a little to one side, with
insulting arrogance, heightened by a sidelong

"'YOU CAN THROW YOUR CLUB AT ME IF YOU CHOOSE TO.'"   Page 81.

look out of his half-shut eyes. "You've come
to get the old lunatic's money. You're welcome! But none of your impudence with
me! I'll let this club drive at your head if
you open it again and let out any of your
sass!"

Andrew, who had been very red, now turned
pale, even to his ears, which seemed to stand
out from his head more like wings than ever.
A natural impulse caused him to step behind
old Nathan's sentry-box, but he did not
stoop. Standing head and shoulders above
that convenient breastwork, he answered,
steadily,—

"You can throw your club at me if you
choose to. That will only go to show that
you are not far from what he says you are."

"What's that?" said the tall swaggerer.

"You know yourselves what you are," replied Andrew, "coming here to rob an old
man's chestnut tree the minute you hear he's
sick! Why don't you come when he's out
with that big cane of his?"

"Ned Burge, don't you throw that!" cried

Phronie, running up just as the club was raised to threaten or to hurl. "You'll get yourself into a worse scrape than you ever did yet!"

"Did ye think I was going to hit him?" returned Ned. "I've as much right here as anybody. Chestnuts are free, wherever you find 'em."

"Not if the owner forbids trespassing," said Andrew. "You've had warning!"

"The old man can't bring a suit. He'd have to get his guardian to bring it for him, and that's my father," said Ned.

"What are you here for, Phronie Wilbur?" called out the second of the Burge brothers, with good-natured familiarity. "I should think you might be in better company."

"I should think *you* might be in better business, Sol Burge! I know how you found out Mr. Petridge was sick. I'm here to do something for him, while you!"— the sentence closed with a look of unutterable disdain.

The marauders did not throw any more clubs, but, after picking up a few nuts by way of bravado, went off munching them, and disappeared over the bank. Andrew remained with Phronie, to pick up the chestnuts left on the ground.

"How did they know I had come, and that the old man was sick?" he asked.

"They got it of Lem Gorbett, one of our drivers. Lem would be a pretty good fellow, if it wasn't for just such bad company as the Burge boys. I should think you would have been afraid!"

"I was afraid," said Andrew, with his dryest intonations. "But I wasn't going to be scared out of my wits by 'em. Now, let me try a club."

"Oh, isn't this perfectly delightful!" cried Phronie, as the nuts came rattling to the ground. "I should like nothing better than to stay and pick up chestnuts all the forenoon; but I must be going home now."

"Must you?" said Andrew, regretfully. "Cleaning windows won't be half so interesting without your help."

It was, in fact, a disagreeable task. He

hated the feeling of the wet rags, and he couldn't help spattering his clothes. Still he kept on, leaving his work only to attend to the wants of the querulous old man. Had he come all the way from Ohio for this?

CHAPTER XIII.

MRS. WILBUR was in no haste to send up
the servant; considering, perhaps, from Phronie's account of Andrew, that he could do the
work without assistance. By noon he was
tired and hungry; and it seemed to him time,
not only to think of dinner, but also to learn
something definite regarding the old man's resources.

"You'll impoverish me!" groaned Nathan,
when Andrew, having got ten cents from him,
asked for more.

"Then your riches are all a sham!" said
Andrew.

"No, no!" Mr. Petridge protested. "But
they are put out of the way; tied up; salted
down. You know what that is."

"I only know that you'll have to untie

85

some of them, if you mean to keep out of
the poorhouse," said Andrew, standing by the
bed and looking dejectedly at the dime in
his palm. "I've no money to speak of, and
Mrs. Wilbur isn't going to give you a broth
every day."

"Since you insist," said the old man, bringing up a few cents more from the depths of
his pocket, as he lay on the bed. "But don't
be extravagant; don't spend everything, because I give up and trust you."

"Everything!" cried Andrew. "Come, if
I am to stay till you get better, I must know
just what you have to live on."

"I didn't think you had come to rob me
like my blood relations!" Nathan complained,
as little by little he emptied his tattered
pockets, in each of which was some small
change, amounting to less than a dollar in all.

"So, this is your immense wealth!" said
Andrew, convinced that he had no more on
his person, whatever his hidden hoards might
be.

"All I have at command, every cent! I'm

like a man with a whole herd of cattle, and not a beefsteak." Old Nathan gave a crafty chuckle as he made use of his favorite comparison.

"Where do you keep your money, if you really have any?" Andrew demanded. "You promised last night to tell me."

"I'll tell you, when I get to know you better," the old man replied, with a sickly, fawning smile; "when I learn to have confidence in you. Then you shall wallow in cash; literally wallow!"

"I don't ask to wallow in it," said Andrew. "But, seriously,"— pressing the paltry sum in his hand, —"this won't do! If you have money salted down, as you say, you must take a little out of the brine. Is it anywhere in the house?"

"No, no; not anywhere in the house!" the old man hastened to declare. "Don't think of looking for it, Nephew Andrew! You'll spoil everything. It's magic money, and you don't know the right hocus-pocus."

"Then I may as well take my valise and go!

exclaimed Andrew. "Here, I don't want any
of your small change." He flung the jingling
handful indignantly down upon the bed, and
started for the attic, where he had left his
valise.

Whether as crazy or not on some points
as he appeared, Nathan Petridge was sane
enough to perceive that Andrew's stay with
him had been prolonged on account of his
own helpless condition, and he had taken
advantage of the discovery. It was pleasant
for him to lie and be waited upon, and to see
the lonesomeness of the old house relieved by
the presence of so tall and strong and useful
a "nephew."

He was, no doubt, weak enough that morning, until Mrs. Wilbur's broth revived him.
When surprised by the announcement that
the Burge boys were at his chestnut tree,
he inadvertently betrayed some returning
strength, but quickly, upon a little reflec-
tion, fell back upon his bed again. Better
lose the chestnuts than his nephew.

Now, however, there seemed to be danger of

losing the nephew anyway; he could hear his
footsteps ascending the carpetless stairs and
treading on the bare boards overhead. He
sprang out of bed, tiptoed in his stockings
across the floor, listened a moment at the foot
of the stairs, and then stole back into the room
with a chuckling laugh, as if he had made up
his mind to do a cunning thing.

If Andrew really meant to carry out his
threat of leaving him, he thought better of
it the moment he was alone. Pity quickly
succeeded to impatience; and he felt he must,
at least, remain until Nathan Petridge was on
his feet again. And now the old man began
to call loudly in the room below.

"See!" he cried, gleefully, holding up something in his skinny fingers as Andrew went
down to him.

It was a bank note, an unrumpled dollar
bill, so fresh and new that it could hardly
have been carried long concealed about his
tattered clothing.

"Stay with me, nephew mine!" he said,
with a fond smile. "Stay till I'm able to

go out and visit my bank, and you shall
wade in bank bills; you shall stand in bank
bills and greenbacks up to your eyes and
ears! I tell you, it's magic money!"

CHAPTER XIV.

THE BAKER, THE BAKERY, AND THE BAKER'S SMALL
ASSISTANT.

"WELL, how are you getting on up there?"
the baker's wife inquired, as Andrew entered
the shop on the afternoon of the following
day.

"Pretty well, I think," he replied, casting
his eyes about wistfully for Phronie, who was
not present. "I've done about all I can for
Mr. Petridge just now. It isn't necessary for
me to be with him all the time, and I — I've
been wondering whether you haven't some
work I can do to pay you for your kindness
to us both."

"Oh, bless me," she cried, tears coming into
her eyes, "don't speak of pay! I've been glad
to do the old man a neighborly turn, and I've
done by you only as I'd have anybody else do
by a boy of mine."

"I'd like to do some work for you," he in-
sisted. "I don't care what it is; errands, or
anything."

As she looked at him, it suddenly occurred
to her that the greatest blessing she could
confer upon this friendless, forlorn boy would
be to give him some employment.

"I shall have to consult my husband," she
said, something which she seemed rather re-
luctant to do.

The truth was, Mr. Wilbur was not so benev-
olent a person as his wife, and what she and
Phronie had already done for Andrew and old
Nathan had caused a domestic cloud. "Leaving me and the shop," he muttered, "to carry
broths and things to an old miser, and to do
favors for a perfect stranger, who may be an
impostor, for aught we know!"

He had not yet seen Andrew, however, and
Mrs. Wilbur hoped he might be more charitably
disposed toward him when he should come
to know what a well-meaning boy he undoubtedly was. He ought at least to be mollified by
Andrew's offer to work for benefits received.

"This way," she said, after some hesitation. "I'll see what he says."

They found Mr. Wilbur at his long, bench-like table, before a window in the back shop; he was bent over a loaf of cake, which he was covering with a coat of white paste, spread on with a knife. The low ceiling was blackened with smoke from the ovens, and covered with flies, and flies were so thick about the loaf he was frosting that he had to use some adroitness to avoid imbedding them in the sweet paste. It was the season of the year which drives flies into houses, and the warmth and odor of the bakery attracted them in swarms.

"This is the young man I spoke to you about," Mrs. Wilbur said to her husband. "He would like any little job of work to pay for what we have done for him and Mr. Petridge."

The baker gave Andrew a glance, and without a word, went on with his frosting. Having coated well his cake, he began to mark it off into narrow parallelograms with the edge of his knife.

"They want it in rather thin slices. I forgot to tell you," said his wife.

Still he made no reply, but went on with his marking. Andrew tried to forget his embarrassment in watching the baker's work. Having covered the cake with two rows of parallelograms, divided by a single stroke of his knife down the middle, each parallelogram representing a future slice, he took from a shelf a short, thick, brass instrument, like a small syringe, and filled it with his white paste.

"He'll speak to you in a minute," the baker's wife said, encouragingly, to Andrew. "I must go back into the front shop."

The baker had an assistant, a boy about twelve years old, who was picking over some raisins at the farther end of the table, slyly tossing one now and then into his mouth after Mrs. Wilbur had gone out. Andrew filled up his time by watching the two. He also took a deliberate survey of the shop, the great kneading-troughs, the wooden trays, the iron pans, the empty barrels, and the general aspect of flour, which encrusted almost everything, from the baker's apron and overalls to the small brass scales and weights standing before him on the table.

At a muttered command from the man, the boy threw open one of the ovens, under the wide, low arch of which, dimly lighted by the glow of an unseen fire, appeared a group of long, black pans, full of white rolls. The baker left his cake to look in at them critically; then taking down from under the ceiling a long-handled, oar-shaped wooden shovel, called a "peel," he thrust the broad blade under one of the pans, and drew it toward him along the smoothly worn fire-brick floor.

He examined the rolls more carefully at the oven's mouth, then shoved the pan back into its place, leaving them to take on a somewhat browner complexion, and returned to his cake.

The boy shut the iron door with a loud clang, and strutting after his master, shook his small fist with comical defiance behind his back, at the same time giving Andrew five or six very rapid and very knowing winks.

Noticing that Andrew's attention was diverted, the baker turned, and would have caught the urchin in the very act of making fun of him if the boy, with a motion almost as swift as one of his winks, had not assumed a serious business air, and returned demurely to his raisins.

CHAPTER XV.

THE baker, apparently forgetful of Andrew's
presence, proceeded with the ornamentation of
his loaf. Pressing the handle of his syringe-
like frosting-machine, and causing a thin
stream of the paste to exude, like a small
white worm, he dabbed it on in little coils and
curls, crossing and recrossing the cake.

At last, without looking up, he spoke, but
not to Andrew.

"Got 'em all sorted?"

"Yes, sir," replied the boy, in a perfectly
respectful tone of voice, making at the same
time an impishly derisive face, for Andrew's
edification, over the baker's bent back.

"Now grease these pans."

"Yes, sir," very deferentially, and, passing
behind his master, the boy made a motion of

97

kicking him over his table and out of the window. As the baker was a well-built man, of considerable breadth of timber, and the boy rather small even for his years, the ludicrousness of the suggestion made Andrew laugh, in spite of the distressing awkwardness of his situation. He coughed to disguise his merriment, and spoke to account naturally for his cough.

"As you are pretty busy, perhaps I had better not wait."

"What was it you wanted?" said the baker. Andrew explained. "What can you do?"

"Almost any common job of work," said Andrew.

"Can you do what he is doing?" Mr. Wilbur referred to the boy, who, at that moment, was performing a series of perfectly frightful contortions of countenance, expressive of his opinion of somebody, accompanying them with pointed flings of his brush-handle in the direction of the worthy baker.

Taking it for granted that the question did not relate to the boy's antics, but to the more

useful exercise of his talents in painting the
inside of the pans with the contents of a grease-
pot, Andrew answered confidently, "I think I
could learn to do that."

"Could you pick over raisins without eating
the plumpest you came across?"

"I think I could do it without eating any at
all."

"Then you could do better than Ike here,"
said the baker, with a glum sort of humor.
"This wedding-cake has got to go to Cambridge
in the morning; can you deliver it?"

"I'm not acquainted in Cambridge, but I
guess I could find my way," said Andrew.

"Yes, and how do I know you wouldn't eat
the cake, and never find your way back again?"
said the baker.

"Maybe it wouldn't be safe to trust me with
anything so tempting as that," Andrew replied,
thinking he might as well treat such a suggestion with levity. "But I might saw and get in
this pile of wood out here."

"No danger of your eating that, eh?" said
the baker, with a twinkle of the eye, turned

up quickly at his visitor, with a more amicable
expression. " Well, come around here in the
morning, and we'll see."

What Andrew had secretly hoped for, when
he first offered his services to Mrs. Wilbur, now
came to pass. He acquitted himself so credita-
bly in the wood-cutting that other jobs were
given him, and instead of working merely to
pay for past favors, he found himself earning
something more.

The business of the bakery was increasing,
and such help as a willing and intelligent lad
could render came, as Mrs. Wilbur declared,
"right handy." He did errands, and learned
the geography of the town ; he was not only
trusted to deliver important orders, including
wedding-cake and other delicacies, but even,
upon occasions, to keep the front shop, make
sales, and receive money.

At first, he obtained his own and old Nathan's food chiefly at the bakery, receiving it
in return for his work. Often Mrs. Wilbur
gave him a bit of steak for his own breakfast,
or a dish of soup at dinner, with something

" warm and comforting " to carry home to the
old man. Then he was made happy by being
given a seat at the family table.

Meanwhile, he found it very convenient to
lodge at Mr. Petridge's. He became attached
to his attic room, and even conceived a sort of
liking for the old man. Nathan gradually
recovered from his bedridden condition, as he
saw Andrew settle down, with apparent con-
tent, to his new way of living. He seemed to
regard his nephew, as he delighted to call him,
with great affection, as well he might, considering his dependence upon him, his own money
being all gone, and his feeble health preventing
him — so he persisted — from visiting his bank.

CHAPTER XVI.

WHY THE BURGE BOYS BROKE INTO AND RANSACKED
OLD NATHAN'S HOUSE IN HIS ABSENCE.

ONE day — he had occasion afterwards to
remember that it was the first day of November — Andrew went up to carry the old man a
plate of pudding from Mrs. Wilbur's table, and
was surprised, as he approached, to hear strange
noises in the house.

Very different they were from those which
had alarmed him on the evening when he went
in and found old Nathan groaning with pain.
There was a noise of pounding.

"What is he up to now?" he wondered,
and was at first inclined to think the old man,
having burnt up his fences, was beginning to
make firewood of the house itself. But there
were voices within, not at all like old Nathan's.
In fact, old Nathan was not there at all; he
had disappeared since morning, and in his place

were two strapping young fellows, hard at work, with their coats off, tearing up the shed floor.

Andrew came upon them suddenly, and watched them for a few moments from the door before they were aware of his presence.

"If it ain't here, then I don't know where it is," said one of them. "These are the only loose boards I can find."

"I don't believe it's in the house at all," said the other. "But we'll make sure."

Andrew recognized Ned and Sol Burge, and quickly guessed their errand.

"What are you doing here?" he cried, just as Sol, perceiving him, gave his brother a poke with his foot, while Ned was stooping to rip up a board.

"No harm," said Sol, laughing, with a bold front. "In pursuit of useful knowledge, that's all."

"I know well enough what you're after," replied Andrew; "and if you don't get out of here at once, I'll go straight and call the police."

"Put the boards back," Ned muttered. "It ain't here."

"No, and it isn't anywhere — certainly not anywhere in this house," said Andrew.

"Oh! you've looked for it, yourself, have you?" sneered Ned, with a jerk of his chin, as he looked up from the floor. "I thought as much."

"Yes, I have; I've watched the old man, and I've looked in every place where it would be possible for him to hide his money. But I did it for his own good, not to rob him."

"We're doing it for his good, too," Ned replied, getting up and striking his fingers together to brush off the dust. "Maybe you don't know it, but we are his relations."

"Yes, I know it well enough. But that gives you no right here." Andrew stood holding his plate of pudding covered by a bowl as he spoke. "If you couldn't find his money after you had put him into the hospital, how do you expect to find it now? I tell you, his being rich is just one of his insane notions, and nothing more."

"If you thought that, would you be stopping

with him here?" Ned retorted. "You're no
such fool. You are after the same thing we're
after. But we have a right to it, and you
haven't."

"But don't think we want to steal it," put
in Sol. "We only want to find where it is."

"So that you can know whether it will pay
to send him to the hospital again," said Andrew. "Where is he now?"

"That's what we'd like to know," Ned answered, with brazen frankness. "He was seen
to take a horse-car at the foot of the street, and
ride towards Charlestown; but he may have
been going through Charlestown to Boston."

"You'd better have followed him; you'd
have stood a much better chance of discovering his hidden riches," said Andrew. They
did not inform him that their younger brother
had gone on that wild-goose chase. But Sol
spoke up: "If he has no money, how does he
pay his rent?"

"For this house? I don't imagine he has
any rent to pay," replied Andrew. "He claims
that he owns it, but that he doesn't dare hold

it in his own name for fear of your taking it
from him. I suppose the real owner is an old
acquaintance who gives him the use of the
premises while the hill is being cut down. Nobody else would live here."

"You suppose what's absurd," said Sol, putting on his coat. "We know who owns the
house, and he ain't a man to give anybody any
rent. Now look here!" addressing Andrew in
a confidential and friendly manner, "find out
where his money is, if you don't know already,
and we'll pay you handsomely for the information."

As Andrew stood amazed at this cool proposal, Ned took up the argument.

"Of course you understand he ain't in a condition of mind to give or will his property
away. Father is his legal guardian. He gave
us authority to come and search the premises.
We've everything in our own hands — only we
haven't. Now, you help us, and we'll do the
fair thing by you."

"We'll give you what he has no right to give
and you've no right to take," Sol added. "If

he should fork out to you a thousand dollars in
gold, it would be stealing for you to pocket a
dollar of it."

"And it is not stealing for you to come and
break into his house, and take anything you
can lay your hands on!" Andrew exclaimed,
full of amazement and indignation. "I'm glad,
for one," he added, "that the property you are
worrying about has no existence, if only that
you may never get it. As for your bribing me
to play into your hands"—he was too angry
to go on.

"You mean to stand in our way?" cried
Ned. "Then look out!" He gave Andrew a
sinister look, with his chin canted and his eyes
half shut. "You won't help us?"

"Go!" shouted Andrew, pointing to the
shed door. And they went.

He found that the house had been ransacked
from top to bottom, and that even the mattress
the old man slept on had been ripped open.

"I should think they might be satisfied
now!" he exclaimed. "The idea that their
father's guardianship over the old man gives

them a right to rummage and plunder in this
style!"

They must have got in by discovering the
key under the back doorstep, where old Nathan
had told Andrew he would hide it, if ever he
should leave the house in his absence. The
doorstep had been overturned, and the key was
in the lock, on the outside of the door.

CHAPTER XVII.

IN WHICH, BY A RARE CHANCE, ANDREW ENJOYS A SIGHT OF MORE OF THE OLD MAN'S MONEY.

AFTER putting the house to rights as well as he could, Andrew left the old man's dinner on the table where he would find it, locked the door, replaced the key under the step, and went back to the bakery. At his work, however, Nathan's absence from home continued to trouble him. He could not wait till night to relieve his anxiety, but having an errand on the streets about four o'clock, took advantage of it to run up the hill.

He was startled to find a solitary horse and buggy standing in the deep dusk, dark against the yellow earth of the caved bank. He peered into the hood of the carriage, and finding it empty, the horse being fastened by a strap and weight, he went on up the bank.

There was a light in the house; that was at

109

least an assurance that Mr. Petridge was there. But who was with him? Andrew, as he drew nigh, could hear him talking in a high, querulous key, which so excited his curiosity that, in passing a window, he stopped to look in.

Himself concealed by the outer shadows, he could see what was going on in the ill-lighted room. On the old pine table the lamp burned dimly. Close by sat a stranger, in a loose overcoat, with a black hat on his head, his left shoulder turned toward the window so that Andrew could see only his side face and thick, gray beard. He sat quietly, with his hand resting on a pile of bank notes, in the full glow of the lamp.

Before him stood old Nathan, talking and gesticulating, with his cane under one arm, and something like a bank note crumpled in his hand.

"It will ruin me!" he was saying. "I have already paid you twice too much."

The stranger said something in a low, decisive tone, and Nathan, with a gesture of despair, threw down his bank note on the table. The

stranger placed it on his pile, and pressed it down with his broad hand.

"No, no! not another dollar!" cried old Nathan. "You can't be so cruel! I've my nephew on my hands now, and I can't afford it."

The stranger seemed to insist, however; whereupon Mr. Petridge, after much violent protestation, walked abruptly into the back entry. Andrew could not tell whether he remained there, or went into the pantry, or into the shed. After an absence of two or three minutes only, he returned, with another bank note in his hand.

As he was still holding on to it, and begging to be let off, the stranger raised his voice in reply, loud enough to be heard by the boy who stood in the darkness behind the panes.

"Come, Nathan! You know I know you have money enough. I must be going before it gets any darker, or I shall break my neck getting down to where I left my buggy."

"It will be a judgment upon you!" cried old Nathan. "You shouldn't be so inhuman in your treatment of an old friend."

With a hard, dry smile, the stranger rose
from the table, and reached out his hand for
the last bank note, which old Nathan finally
yielded, not without contortions of despair.
When all was over, however, he picked up a
paper which lay on the table, smiled, and seemed
suddenly to recover from his distress. He even
took the lamp, in a most obliging way, to show
the visitor to the door, where they met Andrew
coming in.

"My nephew," said Mr. Petridge, introdu-
cing them. "You didn't believe I had such a
nephew, but here he stands. Andrew, this is
my old friend, Mr. Hanks."

Mr. Hanks was in too great a hurry to stop
and talk; he was afraid of the caved bank.
Andrew proposed to help him down.

"Excuse me, Mr. Hanks," he said, having
accompanied him to the edge of the hill. His
voice trembled as he added, "I want to ask you
a plain question."

"Very well; anybody can have that privi-
lege," Mr. Hanks replied, with his dry, but not
unkindly smile, standing there in the last

gleams of daylight. "Answering is another thing."

"I saw something of what passed just now between you and Mr. Petridge," Andrew resumed.

"Ah!" replied Mr. Hanks, quietly. "Then you saw him give me some money."

"Yes, very much to my surprise!" said Andrew. "I didn't believe he had any."

"It seems he has enough to pay his rent."

"And you" —

"I am the man he pays it to. I am the owner of this confounded hill they are cutting off. He don't pay much, but he can well afford to pay a little, though it's like pulling his eye-teeth — if he had any eye-teeth left to pull. Thank you," as Andrew helped him down to the grade of the highway. "I'm afraid you don't have a very good time living with him in the old house."

"I don't much mind, for my own part. But if he has money he ought to be made to use it for his own comfort. Has he much?"

"Oh dear!" Mr. Hanks replied, laughing at

the boy's earnestness, as he lifted his carriage weight by the strap and put it into the buggy. "That's what some other people are in a stew to find out, and I'm happy to answer, I don't know. Nor where he keeps it, nor anything at all about it, except that he pays his rent twice a year. That's where my interest in his business begins and ends. Good-night, my young friend."

And, settling down comfortably into his buggy, with a heavy lap-robe wrapped about his legs, the owner of the " confounded hill" rode away.

CHAPTER XVIII.

HOW LEM GORBETT STEPPED DOWN FROM THE BAKER'S
WAGON, WHILE HIS SUCCESSOR STEPPED UP.

MR. PETRIDGE remained as poor as ever after
this. Paying his rent, he said, had exhausted
his ready resources, though he still talked of
imaginary millions.

Andrew had learned that argument with a
mind so manifestly disordered led to no satis-
factory results. But he was convinced that
Nathan had a little money; and by urgent in-
sistence he succeeded in getting small sums
from him now and then.

With these, and with what he himself earned
at the bakehouse, he was able to provide for
him quite comfortably during the following
winter. The old man's sentry box was re-
stored to its former use as a coal bin, and
Andrew made him keep a good fire in the
stove; he also brought in other necessaries; so

115

that the old house was rendered habitable in the cold weather.

He owed much to the advice and sympathy of Mrs. Wilbur and Phronie, and the substantial assistance they gave him.

Mr. Wilbur's bark was worse than his bite, his wife said; and she did not let his remonstrances cut off the stream of her benefits. Andrew, meanwhile, made himself so useful that the baker continued to give him employment, while regarding him with suspicion and dislike.

Lem Gorbett, friend of the Burge boys, and driver of one of the baker's wagons, was likewise aggrieved by the favor shown to Andrew by the women folks; and he managed to fan their employer's jealousy. Andrew felt deeply the unjust opposition of these two. But he consoled himself with the principle of conduct which his mother's letter had taught him. Whatever happened, he resolved to be patient and bide his time.

The winter was past, and it was April when Mrs. Wilbur told Andrew, one morning, that as

he had a little leisure he might get on Lem's
wagon with him, and see something of the
neighboring towns.

"I want you to get better acquainted," she
said to Lem, "and be better friends." But
what she said to her husband was this:

"You know very well, Lem's habits are not
good, that he keeps bad company, Ned and Sol
Burge, for instance, and you may be obliged to
discharge him any day. You've said so yourself. But he thinks he has us in his power, because nobody else knows his routes. Now, I'm
determined to have some one to put into his
place, when we find we can't stand his ways
any longer. Andrew is just that one."

"Oh, of course!" replied the baker, with
heavy sarcasm. "Andrew! Andrew! it's always Andrew! You make a fool of that boy!"

Yet he did not absolutely forbid her putting
Andrew on to learn Lem's routes. The result
proved her foresight. It was not many weeks
before Lem's dissipations culminated in a night's
frolic which unfitted him for appearing at the
shop at the usual hour the next morning.

It was ten o'clock before he finally came round, swaggering and insolent, and demanded what had become of his horse. He had been at the stable and missed him.

"Your horse?" cried the baker's wife. "The horse you have been driving, and the wagon, too, are in safer hands than yours. And I guess we can dispense with your services in future."

"Is that so, Mr. Wilbur?" Lem appealed, in a humble tone, to the baker.

"That's about the way it looks," Mr. Wilbur replied, siding with his wife for once. In fact, with all his grumbling and fretting, he usually followed her advice in matters of importance. "We can't have you coming to business this time of day, if you work for us."

"But you'll allow," pleaded Lem, "I've never been so late before."

"Perhaps not quite. But you've often come when you were not fit to get on to your wagon and drive a horse. You've had warnings enough, Lem Gorbett."

Lem still hoped to have the wagon again

the next day, and he lingered about the bake-house, trying to get back into favor. He only succeeded, however, in getting some occasional employment, in Andrew's place, while Andrew kept the wagon.

Andrew did not pretend to know much about horses; he had never had the care of one be-fore. He liked it, however; he enjoyed the freedom of his new occupation, his rides, often in the open country, in the beautiful spring weather, his chats with customers, and, not least, his increased wages.

"He may bring in as much money as I did," Lem would say; "he can't very well help that. You know what he takes out, and what he ought to bring in. Any one, though, with half an eye, can see he don't know how to take care of a hoss. He don't keep Dicky brushed down as I did; and he's falling away in flesh."

CHAPTER XIX.

NOBODY else could see that the animal was
not as well curried now as when Lem had him.
But along in June it became apparent, not only
that his ribs were growing prominent, but that
his spirit and strength were failing. Andrew
himself was the first to perceive that Dicky no
longer got over the track with lightness and
ease, as when he first took him, but that he required more and more urging.

"Are you sure you feed him well?" the
baker asked, seeing the horse come in jaded
one evening.

"I'm very sure. I give him a measure of
grain night and morning, just as you directed,"
replied Andrew; "and fill his rack with hay.
His appetite is good, he eats up everything
clean. And I water him regularly."

120

"**Well, increase** his feed a little," said the baker.

This Andrew did, but without putting **flesh** on the horse's ribs. There would be days when the animal would show **a** little more vigor in making his rounds; but **on the whole there was** no improvement.

"**I'm** afraid I shall **have to put away that** beast," Mr. Wilbur at length said, dubiously shaking his head, as he watched Andrew **start** off on one of his daily trips.

"Better put away the driver," replied **Lem.** "He **don't** know any more about a hoss than **a** frog does **about a** fiddle. **See how** he holds the reins!"

"I don't **see** but what **he holds the** reins as well as anybody," interposed the baker's wife, as she came to the door. "And why should he neglect the horse? **He** declares **he** don't, and I believe him. There's something the matter with Dicky."

"Here's Towner," **said Lem.** "Ask his opinion."

Towner was the driver **of** the other wagon.

Each driver took care of his own horse, and
had nothing to do with the other. Towner was
a middle-aged man, of few words, friendly
enough to both Lem and Andrew, but inclined
to take sides with his old associate against the
new-comer.

"It's plain enough," he said, when his judgment was appealed to, "that Dicky don't have
just the care he did when Lem drove him. I
don't know why it is; must be Andrew don't
feed him reg'lar. And I notice Dicky laps up
his oats in a quarter the time the General does.
I never saw a hoss eat so quick as he does
lately. As if he was 'mos' starved."

"Do you think you could take Dicky and
build him up again?" the baker asked.

Towner guessed he could if anybody could,
but he didn't care to try.

"But I want you to try. I want you to
drive Dicky and let Andrew take the General,
till we see if changing masters will make the
difference Lem claims it will."

This was not just the change Lem hoped
for; neither did it suit Towner. He didn't

fancy the idea of giving up the sleek General to Andrew, and taking a run-down nag in his place.

Andrew was likewise chagrined. But Dicky's unaccountable falling away had so perplexed him, that he was ready to accept any arrangement that promised to explain the mystery.

To his great surprise, but I fear not quite so much to his gratification, Dicky began to pick up very soon after he passed into Towner's hands. Everybody noticed it; Lem crowed over it; and Andrew could not deny it. Fortunately, the General did not at the same time show signs of failure.

But something else happened, even more startling, late in the summer. The General ran away! To have a horse run away with a baker's wagon, and the pies and cakes and loaves and rolls that fill its lidded chests and case of drawers, is about as undesirable as any small accident that can be imagined.

Andrew did not know how it came about. He had left the General at the corner of a Somerville street, while he went to call upon a cus-

tomer near by ; he was detained a few minutes,
and when he came out of the house, horse and
wagon were gone. He ran to the corner in
time to see a drawer which he had left unfas-
tened, dropping out of the end of the wagon,
followed quickly by another, scattering their
tarts, pies, and jelly-cakes as the horse tore
away up the street.

There was nobody near to tell what had
frightened him, and Andrew did not stop to
inquire. He followed, picking up the drawers
by the way, but leaving their contents on the
pavement, and kept on, in wild pursuit, expecting nothing less than that the wagon would be
dashed to pieces and the General ruined.

The catastrophe was not so bad as it might
have been, had the General been a less steady
and sensible horse. He avoided obstacles in
his course, and slackened his speed as he got
farther away from the real or fancied danger
that had startled him ; and finally turned up to
the side door of the bakery, where he stopped.
There Andrew found him, surrounded by a
group of spectators, when, flushed and breath-

less and frightened, he came running, with an
empty drawer in each hand, to learn the extent
of the damage.

Phronie hastened to meet him; she and her
mother had been far more anxious about him
than about anything that might have happened
to the horse and wagon.

"Don't mind! It's lucky you didn't have a
smash-up," she said, reassuringly.

But how could he help minding? He didn't
see how he was to blame, and yet he knew he
would be blamed; and it was with a sense of
something very much like guilt that he approached the wondering group, panting for
breath, and lugging the drawers.

"I'm glad you've brought back a whole
neck!" exclaimed Mrs. Wilbur, cheerfully, as
she finished examining the shaken-up contents
of the wagon. But the baker demanded, in
his surliest tones: "What do you say to this?"

"I — don't know — what to say," Andrew
gasped out. Then, as he gained breath, he
went on to relate all he knew of the affair.
The spectators generally appeared friendly.

Lem Gorbett was not there to jeer at him; only the boy, Ike, seemed to find much fun in the accident.

"Well!" growled the baker, "take him and finish your round, if you think you can be trusted; such a boy as you ain't fit to have the management of a horse, anyway! Now we'll see what will happen next."

If Lem had been on the spot, there is no doubt but he would then and there have been put upon the wagon in Andrew's place. But, the crisis over, Mrs. Wilbur prevailed upon her husband to give the unlucky Andrew still another trial.

CHAPTER XX.

IT was for **the most** part a cash business, so that **he had** daily the handling of small sums. But Mr. Wilbur had a few bills out; there was also a grocer in Medford whom he had assisted, and who **was** making **prompt quarterly payments** of his **debt.**

Early in October **Andrew was** commissioned to collect one of the **Medford** man's payments, together with **a few** other bills due **on** his route. So **he** returned home that afternoon with an unusual amount of money — one hundred **and** eight dollars — in **what he** called his "roadbook."

This was made for memoranda and bankbills, and was fastened by a rubber band. **He** commonly carried it, for convenience, **in** the side pocket of his coat; **a safe** enough place

127

under ordinary circumstances. But he had
never before been entrusted with so much
money at a time, and it made him more than
commonly cautious. So he put it into his inside breast-pocket, and buttoned his coat over
it tightly.

He had also another commission to execute
that afternoon. Phronie wanted two or three
ripe milkweed pods for some ornamental purpose, and had asked him to bring them home
to her, if he should see any by the way. He
had picked some on a hillside in Medford, and
placed them loose in the side pocket where he
usually carried his road-book.

He remembered that it was a year that day
since he arrived at the old house on the hill,
and made his first visit to the baker's shop.
The recollection caused him to think of many
things on his homeward ride; his strange experience with old man Petridge, the kindness of
Phronie and her mother, the way in which his
present occupation seemed to have been shaped
for him, almost without any choice of his own,
and how he had been prospered in spite of the

opposition of others. His mind went back .to
that dreary night in the old house, when he
read his mother's letter, and took in for the
first time its full significance; and forward to
the future, which was beginning to look bright
to him, though so different from what he had
anticipated when he made his rash Eastern journey in answer to old Nathan's letter of invitation.

Occupied with these thoughts, the homeward
drive seemed short to him; and yet it was
nearly dark when he turned into the narrow
lane, at the end of which, not far from the shop,
stood the barn where the baker kept his wagons
and horses. Towner's wagon was already in,
and Dicky was champing hay in his stall.

Andrew drove his wagon in beside the other,
felt the road-book secure, and assured himself
that Phronie's milkweed pods were whole,
anticipating the satisfaction of soon handing
the money to the mother, and of showing the
daughter that he had not forgotten her request.

He got down from the wagon, detached the
General, unharnessed him, and, with a kindly

slap, sent him through a side door to his stall in the adjoining stable. His stall was the farthest; next to that was Dicky's; then there was an unoccupied stall near the door, containing a pile of litter for bedding.

He followed the General in, made him fast, and saw that there was hay in his rack; then returned to close the huge barn door, and bolt it on the inside, before going out through a smaller door from the stables.

The closing of the big door shut out what was left of the daylight, and he was groping his way to the smaller door, when he heard a rustling of litter which could not have been made by the horses. He paused a moment to listen; then, thinking there was a cat in the stable, he started again for the door. But just as he did so, something big and tremendous flapped over and down upon him, like an enormous wing.

"Ho! What's this?" he shouted, in the sudden fright it gave him, and with the folds of a heavy horse blanket swiftly closing about and stifling his outcry,

He struggled with all his might to cast it off,

and free his face and hands, but something clasped it close, and held it down, and crushed him under it, and bore him, still struggling and uttering muffled cries, to the ground.

Overpowered and deprived of breath, he almost lost consciousness of what was taking place; but he was aware of struggling still, feebly and ineffectually, and of trying to shriek for help, while strong hands held and choked him, and rifled his pockets. Then there was a blank.

When he came to himself, he was lying on the stable floor, gasping for breath, with the blanket wrapped closely about his head, breast, and arms. He quickly remembered that some terrible thing had happened to him, and made an effort to free himself. That was not easily done. The blanket was tied on.

He succeeded in getting an arm out, and sat up, with the frightful encumbrance still over his head and chest. His one free hand now freed the other; they found and loosened a rope halter twisted around the blanket, and flung off all together.

Then, sitting in the darkness on the stable floor, he clutched his breast, only to find his coat torn open, and the road-book gone.

"I've been robbed!" he cried aloud, in despair, as he felt again and again in his pockets, and struggled blindly to his feet.

He had one faint hope ; the book might have fallen out in the tussle, and got lost in the litter of the floor.

By the door hung a lantern, which he had not thought it necessary to light until he should return later to the stable, to bed the General and give him his oats; but now, with shaking nerves, he struck a light, and, lantern in hand, his hat gone, his hair tumbled over his eyes, he stooped and poked, and stifled fierce, dry sobs.

The struggle had taken place between the unoccupied stall and the door. There lay Andrew's hat, which he picked up, and shook, and put on his head. There was the horse-blanket still entangled in the rope ; this he also shook and flung aside. And there was a light sprinkling of loose straw, but no pocket-book.

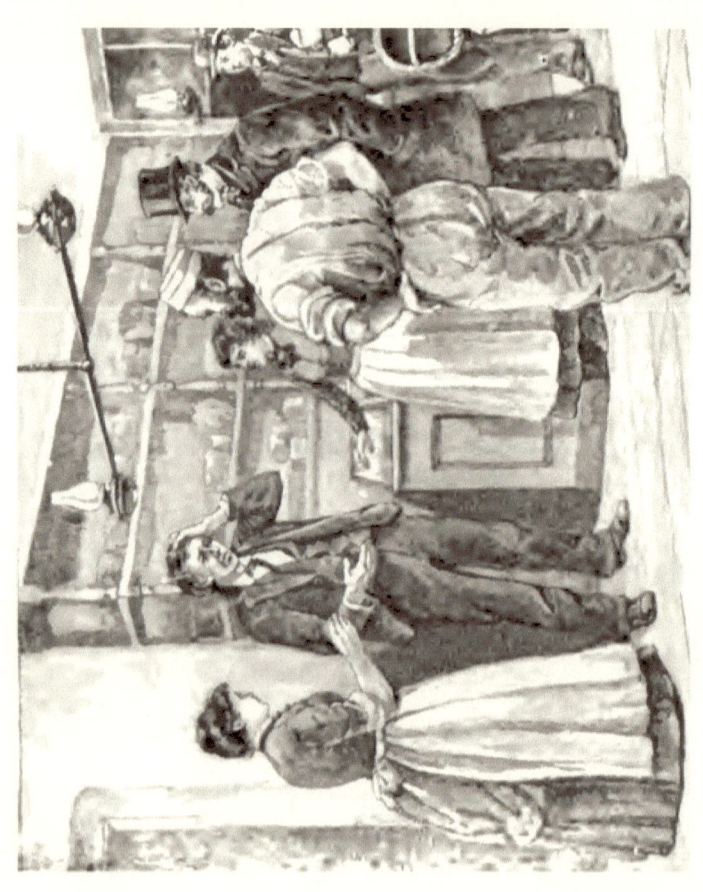

CHAPTER XXI.

"GRACIOUS me, Andrew Hapnell! What's the trouble?"

This exclamation burst from Mrs. Wilbur, when the boy, having entered the rear shop and found nobody, went forward and presented himself, with haggard features and disordered dress, in the salesroom.

"I've been robbed," he said, huskily, but so quietly that the announcement seemed wholly incredible.

"Robbed! How? Of what?" cried the baker's wife.

"Of that money," he replied. "It was taken from me just now in the stable."

In a minute he was surrounded by the whole family, the baker, Mrs. Wilbur, Phronie, and two or three customers. He, the centre of the excited group, appeared the calmest of all, but

133

with the calmness of exhaustion and stupefaction.

"How much money?" Mr. Wilbur demanded, his sparkling eyes scanning the miserable lad from head to foot. Andrew explained.

"Was any of your money taken?"

"No; I left my money at home, all but a little change I had in my pocket. They didn't take the change."

"They? Who?"

"How should I know?"

"Did you chase them?"

"How could I, when they left a horse-blanket tied over my head?"

"Did you yell?"

"Of course I did, or tried to, till they choked the yell out of me." Something of Andrew's peculiar drawl, which he had mostly got rid of, came into his tones as he said this, and gave a humorous turn to his words, though he had never in his life felt so little like making fun.

"Did you run to the door and call help, the first thing?" Mrs. Wilbur asked, while Phronie laughed hysterically.

"No; I suppose I ought to; but it was too late then. I stopped to look for the road-book."

"And you're sure it ain't in the stable?" said the baker.

"Not unless it got into the pile of straw in the vacant stall, and I don't see how that could be," Andrew replied.

"Let's go and see!" said the baker, severe almost to savageness. It was clear enough that he did not believe a word of Andrew's story. "Where's Lem?"

"He came in from the back shop a few minutes before Andrew did, to say he was going for his supper," Phronie replied. "He was putting on his coat."

"And Ike?"

"He's out doing errands."

"You'll have to go yourself then, Phronie, and bring a policeman," said the father, "while I go with Andrew to the barn, and look into the matter, if there's such a thing as looking into it."

Andrew explained again on the spot, as

clearly as he could, to Mr. Wilbur and others who accompanied them to the barn, and afterwards to the policeman who came with Phronie, how the robbery had taken place, and why he acted as he did. He faltered in his replies to a few questions; much remained confused in his mind, and some of the reasons he gave for his conduct seemed to himself so insufficient that he tried to think of better ones.

The truth is, one hardly knows what his own actions and motives are in such a crisis of surprise and fright, and he must have a clearer head than the most of us possess who can afterwards give a straightforward account of things. Thus it happens that the most innocent person will sometimes stammer and forget, while the tale told by the rogue will flow with persuasive smoothness.

Unfortunately, Andrew saw yawning before him the danger of not being believed. A Charlestown clerk had lately been convicted of robbing himself, in order to defraud his employers; a notorious case, still in everybody's mind. He felt the horror of being suspected of playing the same miserable trick, and this made him appear even too anxious to clear himself.

The barn was well back from the street, but not far from other barns and houses, and it seemed that he might have made himself heard at the time of the assault. His assailants could have escaped in the obscurity, by another street in the rear, but it appeared strange that he did not run out and try at least to discover them the moment he was free, instead of waiting to light a lantern and look for the pocket-book.

There were signs of a scuffle on the littered floor, but nothing which Andrew might not have made himself in order to corroborate his story.

When asked if he had any idea who the guilty parties were, he stammered again, and then was silent. He thought he could guess who they were; but he had no proof, and dared not mention names, lest he might be still further suspected of trying to implicate others in order to screen himself.

But he was sure there were two robbers, if not three, and that one of them was tall, with long arms, and very strong. Persons living in the nearest houses were questioned, but nobody had heard any disturbance in the barn, and no suspicious characters had been seen there.

It was late when the matter was finally left in the hands of the police, and the baker's family went in to supper.

"You are coming, too?" Phronie said to Andrew, as he lingered outside the door.

" Why, yes, of course he is coming!" Mrs. Wilbur exclaimed. " Why not, Andrew?" She spoke kindly, but he felt that even she doubted his truth.

"I can't eat anything," he replied, looking a picture of wretchedness, as he hung back and saw the rest go in. And, indeed, his lack of appetite was no pretence. The scuffle, the fall, the excitement and exhaustion, still more perhaps the ordeal of questions and explanations he had gone through, had left him sick in body and soul.

"Come, Andrew!" Phronie stayed to entreat him. "Don't take it so to heart. It will all turn out right."

"I hope it will. If it don't, I — I don't see how I am to blame; but if others blame me " — His feelings were mastering him, and he hastened to change the subject. "I am sorry the milkweed pods I had picked for you got crushed in the scuffle; but I will get you some more the first chance I have."

"Oh, don't mention them!" cried Phronie, in great distress. "I am so sorry, Andrew! Do come in!"

"I really can't," he replied, dropping a tear or two. "I have a headache. I'll see you in the morning; I shall be better then."

"Oh, I hope you will! I know it has been terrible to you. Good-night, Andrew!"

She, at least, believed in him; but why should she? He was half inclined to lose faith in himself. The whole affair of the robbery seemed sickeningly unreal to him. Yet there was the coat torn out at the buttonhole, the empty breast pocket, the milkweed pods crushed to husks and feathers in his side pocket, and the dreadful headache.

CHAPTER XXII.

ANDREW, after a miserable night, returned
to business in more cheerful spirits in the
morning. He went first to the barn, intending to give the General his breakfast before
taking his own, but was stopped at the door,
by Ike, who ran calling after him, —

"You don't drive to-day. Lem's going to
drive."

Although Andrew had half expected this,
it went to his heart like an arrow. Lem was
there before him, whistling in the barn.

"Ike," Andrew said, "I've always been a
friend to you, haven't I? At least, I've meant
to be; and though you've plagued me sometimes, with your nonsense, I think you've been
a friend to me."

"Course I have," Ike answered, in so
strange a tone, and appearing to regard him

140

with such aversion, that Andrew's heart sank.
Even Ike believed him guilty.

"I was going to ask you something, but no
matter; another time," and he walked on behind the boy, to the bakehouse.

He was prepared for what Mr. Wilbur had
to say to him. The baker met him in the
bakeshop, with cold, stern looks.

" Ike told you what I said ? "

"Yes, sir; Lem takes the team, to-day."

"Exactly," said the baker. "We've had
enough of your style of driving."

After a pause, Andrew said, in a choking
voice, "Then I suppose you have nothing for
me to do ? "

"Only one thing," said the baker. "Find
that money."

" But — how — I don't know anything about
it!" Andrew protested.

"Find that money!" the baker repeated, in
a harsh tone. "Then come back to me. Not
before."

Andrew turned to go without a word; he
was so overcome by the monstrous injustice of

which he was the victim, that he felt it would break his heart to speak. Twenty-two dollars of his pay was still due him, but he could not ask for it. The baker called him back.

"Take my advice, Hapnell. We've been good friends to you here, and I speak as a friend now. For your own sake, before it is too late, bring back that money, and make a clean breast of it."

Andrew stood staring in a stupor of dumb distress. The friendly Mr. Wilbur went on.

"It's a preposterous story you tell; I think so, and the police think so, too. Nobody believes there was any robbery. You know where that money is, and I say again, take my advice before it is too late."

"Mr. Wilbur," Andrew at last found voice to reply, "I have told you the truth as well I could. And now, if you mean to turn me out in this way, after you — after Mrs. Wilbur" —

He could say no more, but went out, struggling manfully to repress the wrenching sobs that heaved and broke up his voice.

Andrew did not go back to the house on the hill. There was nothing for him there; old man Petridge could give him neither counsel nor comfort.

He had a few acquaintances in the place, but no intimate friends. There was only one person to whom he wished to pour out his heart. That was Phronie Wilbur. She, at least, — so he hoped, — would give him trust and sympathy; but he could not go to her after being so ruthlessly turned out of doors by her father.

To collect his thoughts, to master his feelings, to get out of sight of everybody who knew him, he walked fast and far. The morning was beautiful; the wayside maples were gorgeous; distant woods flamed like subdued fires in veils of smoke and haze. Gradually, he recovered his firmness of mind, and recalled the philosophical resolutions with which he had begun the day.

In the lonely suburbs, he struck a railroad track, and reflected that it would lead him to Boston. Growing beside it, he saw a cluster

of dry milkweed stalks, bearing aloft their
ripened pods on curiously contorted stems.
A great heart-sickness came over him, as he
remembered the desire and hope with which
he gathered those pods for Phronie, the day
before, and, turning away his face, he hurried
on.

But then he said, "I promised to get her
some more," and retraced his steps. He had
that morning cleared his pocket of the broken
pods, and the adhesive silky down, and into
it he put half-a-dozen more of the most perfect ones he could find.

Then he walked again; he walked to Boston, and walked the streets all day, seeking
for employment, but finding none. His spirit
rose above all discouragement. "I can
walk," he said; "I can walk all the way back
to Ohio, if I get nothing to do here."

He sat down to rest on a bench by the Frog
Pond, before starting for home. Home! With
that old man? He wondered how he had
continued to live with him so long· and what
would become of them both, if he could get

no work. " A poor prospect for A. H. ! " he
said to himself, with set lips.

The Common was lovely in its autumnal
hues. Through the glowing tree-tops, softened
bars of sunlight slanted to the rippling and
dazzling water. Merry youngsters were sail-
ing their toy ships across from curb to curb.
Andrew was looking listlessly about him, seeing, yet not seeing, with intense preoccupation
of mind, when a singular circumstance recalled him abruptly to himself.

His roving eyes lighted by chance on an
evening paper which a stranger was reading,
on the bench beside him, and stopped at a
column of " Suburban Items." The heading
of the first paragraph fixed his attention.

" WAS IT A ROBBERY ? "

As his eye glanced down the lines, he ceased
to be Andrew Hapnell; he became a living,
quivering embodiment of consternation, anger
and shame. For there, in about two stickfuls
(in printers' phrase), some witty reporter told
the story of his adventure of the night before,

giving names in full, but getting Andrew's
ludicrously **wrong** ("Andrew Happenill!"),
and twisting facts **about, to make** them **as lively**
reading as possible. A probable negative an-
swer to the **question,** "**Was it a** robbery?"
was plainly enough implied, **the writer** adding
in the conclusion, —

"**The** police are diligently looking **for** clues,
but no arrests have been **made."**

The stranger folded **his** paper, and put it
into his pocket, **little** knowing that **the** hero
of that paragraph, which he smiled at, was
sitting **on** the **bench, and** reading it over his
shoulder.

CHAPTER XXIII.

OLD NATHAN EATS CHESTNUTS **AGAIN**, WITH **RESULTS** OF VERY GREAT IMPORTANCE TO HIMSELF AND HIS **NEPHEW.**

As Andrew entered, that evening, the door of the old house on the hill, he was smilingly met by the old man; but Nathan's countenance fell when he saw that the boy had come empty-handed, for he usually brought up something from the bakery at that hour.

"Well," said the old man, "what are we to have for supper?"

"I haven't been at the bakehouse since morning," Andrew replied. "I am not going there any more. I am out of work and very nearly out of money."

He sat down wearily on a chair by the table, on which the lamp was burning. The old man was more willing to burn oil since it was supplied by his nephew, at no expense to himself.

147

"But what are we to do?" cried the old man.

"Do? We shall go hungry, I suppose, unless I can find work, or you will be a little more liberal with your millions."

Nathan had continued to hand out small sums now and then, but had never yet revealed the source of them; and Andrew, as long as he was earning money enough for both, cared little for the old man's. "Something has happened," the boy added, gloomily, "which I fear will prevent my getting any more work about here, and I may have to go back to Ohio."

"You mean to desert me!" cried the old man, taking alarm. "I'll be liberal. You shall draw freely on my riches, and I — I'll give you my cane!"

"You've given me that two or three times before," said Andrew.

"But you've never appreciated the present. It is a wonderful relic. Staff made of the rail of the house Dr. Franklin was born in. The head is a piece of the frigate *Constitution*.

The ferrule was a Spanish dollar given to my father by Lafayette, for holding his horse one day, when he was on his visit to this country."

Andrew had heard this story, too, or something like it, several times before, but had regarded it as one of the old man's queer fancies. Once the staff was a piece of a pillory that used to stand on Boston Common; the head was something else, and the dollar had been given by President John Quincy Adams.

"It's real silver," the old man went on, "though you may not think so; and it's yours. Only don't abandon a poor old man in his hour of need!"

He actually extended the cane towards Andrew, but quickly drew it back when Andrew reached out his hand for it.

"When I am through with it," he said, with a crafty grin.

Again the next day he tramped the Boston streets in the hope of finding something to do. It was a disheartening quest; he would much more gladly have turned his face the other way, and begun his long foot journey back to Ohio;

but he could not make up his mind to quit the old man, whom he had made so much more comfortable during his stay than he had been for years, or could be again without him.

Release was near, however, with freedom to set off on that longer, wearier tramp facing the Western sun.

Returning home in the afternoon of that second day, he found a strange group in the house. Nathan Petridge was in the midst of it, but not of it. He was lying dead on his bed, and his nephew by blood relationship, Mr. Soloman Burge, had already taken possession.

Andrew was conscience-smitten. He had left the old man on short rations that day, because he himself was so nearly out of money, and it was necessary to compel a contribution from the secret fund. The result was that Nathan had probably eaten chestnuts, which were again in season, and had died in one of his fits of indigestion.

He had had so many of these spasms since Andrew had known him, always expecting to die in each attack, that the boy had ceased to be frightened by them ; and now he had been carried off by one at last.

Andrew learned that somebody had come to the house and found him dying, and had sent for a doctor and called in other neighbors, so that the elder Burge had heard the news, and come also, bringing with him an old woman to take charge of the house, and look out for his interests. The belief in a hidden treasure was still held by the old man's relations, and it was their policy not to leave Andrew alone in the house a moment after his death.

CHAPTER XXIV.

THE person who had found him dying, and had given the alarm, was Mrs. Wilbur. Her large, motherly heart yearned toward the cast-off boy. She pitied him if innocent, pitied him even more if guilty, and longed to talk with him again. Her own misgivings and Phronie's importunities gave her no peace until she had made him a visit. But she had come and gone, and Andrew was deprived of the consolation of knowing why she had come.

"She spoke of having some things in the house, which she lent you and Uncle Nathan," said Mr. Burge. "I'll thank you to point them out."

The thrifty housekeeper had indeed bethought her to speak in season of those things,

152

"HE WENT FOR THE LAST TIME OUT OF THAT OLD HOUSE."

in order to save them from the well-known ra-
pacity of **Nathan's lawful** heirs. But the thick-
set, gross-featured man put the case in a way
that made Andrew think that had been her
sole business in coming to the house. As if,
now that she trusted him no longer, she were
in anxious haste to get back her loans.

"I will see to them," said Andrew. "And
I suppose," he added, "there is no use of my
staying any longer."

"I don't see any use in it," Mr. Burge replied, with stony coldness.

The sheets on his own bed and one of the
blankets belonged to Mrs. Wilbur. To these
he added a pair of blankets which he had
bought with his own money, and putting all
into one big bundle, together with everything
else he had had of her, even including a pair of
handkerchiefs, he tied them up, ready for the
expressman. Then he put his milkweed pods
in a paper box, which he had brought from
Boston for the purpose; and scribbled a few
lines, which he tucked under the string tied
around it. This is what he wrote : —

" Phronie, here are the milkweed pods I
promised you. I send them along with the
bundle of other things. Tell your mother that
I send a few of my own things, because I have
no more use for them, here or anywhere. I
don't suppose it will be pleasant for any of you
to see me again, thinking of me as you do, at
least some of you, though I did hope, you,
Phronie, knew me better. I am not running
away; I am ready to stand the consequences of
anything I ever did in my life. But I am going away. I start out to find work of some
kind, and shall probably make my way back to
Ohio. I am sick of cities and city life.

" Tell your mother not to think I do not
thank her, and you, too, Phronie, for all your
kindness to me. I do thank you both. It may
be a long while before your father will know
how unjustly he has treated me. But I believe
he will learn the truth some day. I can bide
my time."

Then Andrew packed his little red valise,
and smiled to think he had only about the same
amount of clothing worth taking away, as he
had brought with him from Ohio, and even less
money.

What had his year been worth to him?

But he did not repine. Old clothes had been
replaced by new; old habits of thought by fresh

experiences; narrow views of life by a larger
and fuller knowledge.

When all was ready, he gave a last tearful
look around the old attic, which had somehow
become dear to him, and with a big sigh, valise
in hand, descended the crooked stairs. Only
Mr. Burge and the woman he had placed in
charge remained in the room below. Andrew
would have avoided facing them if he could;
but he did not wish to steal away.

"Off?" said Mr. Burge, with a darkly suspicious look at the boy's valise.

"I can't do anything more for *him*." He
glanced tremulously at the bed where the little
shrivelled old man lay. "That's about all I've
been staying for the past year."

"Huh!" Not a word of thanks from Mr.
Burge, for all Andrew had done for his dead
relative, only a swinish grunt. And he still
eyed the red valise.

"Perhaps you would like to see what I am
carrying out of the house," said Andrew.
"I'll turn everything inside out for you, even
to my empty pockets."

"No," grumbled Mr. Burge. Andrew was
quite too willing.

He gave a last look at the pinched, wrinkled,
and pallid face on the pillow, wearing even in
death such a smile of craft and conceit as he
had often seen upon it in life. Then with his
valise, and a heavy but resolute heart, he
went for the last time out of that old house
on the hill.

He found the youngest of the Burge boys
clubbing the chestnut tree. The sight filled
him with indignant scorn.

"But never mind," he said to himself.
"The old man doesn't care who gets his chestnuts now."

The same wonderful world spread about him,
which he beheld when he first climbed that hill
a year before, — the suburban fields and streets,
the distant cities, the gleams of water, and the
far-off heights, veiled or half veiled by the
October smoke and haze; and here a train of
cars flying through the landscape, with its long,
vaporous plume. Yet what a different world
it was to him now!

He avoided the bakery, but showed himself openly in the town, going first to the express office, to leave an order for the removal of Mrs. Wilbur's effects; then began his long tramp over the hills, with his face toward the sunset, little knowing how or when or where it was to end.

CHAPTER XXV.

IT was not until the next morning that the
expressman brought Mrs. Wilbur her bundle,
and Phronie her box of milkweed pods and letter. That the young girl had a good cry over
her share, we may well believe. To think that
the wronged Andrew, for she had really never
once doubted him, should in the midst of his
trouble remember his promise to her, and take
the pains to gather and send to her those
worthless pods, which she cared nothing for
now, and could not bear to look upon again!

And yet, those worthless things suddenly assumed an undefined value in her eyes. Poor
little pitiful pods, with their soft brown seeds
enclosed, so marvellously arranged around their
folded silken wings, which they covered and
concealed until the hour for escape should ar-

rive! She had not the heart to open one of them. She would keep them to remember Andrew by, if she should never see him again.

Mrs. Wilbur did not cry, as Phronie did; but she was filled with pangs of remorse at the sight of the sheets and blankets and handkerchiefs coming back.

"Why did he send *these?*" she exclaimed, her large heart heaving with its woes. "But perhaps he was right. He knew I half suspected him. I did, for a time. The more fool I! But I don't now. Oh, we must send for him and have him back!"

But where send? Mrs. Wilbur went again up to the old house. But it was a fruitless errand. The woman in charge knew nothing of Andrew, except that he had gone off the evening before.

"It convinces *me* he has got that money," said the baker, when told of Andrew's departure. "Or it *would* convince me, if I wasn't convinced before. Such a robbery as he invented was simply impossible."

And yet Mr. Wilbur himself, as he afterwards confessed, had secret qualms as to the very points about which he was so positive. Though of a surly and jealous disposition, he meant always to be just; and what if he had not been just to Andrew?

He didn't like Lem Gorbett in Andrew's place, now he had got him back. What was there in Lem's manner, as he went whistling to his work, that filled him with misgivings and disgust? Lem did not always whistle in that way.

Andrew had been gone three days, and was many miles away; and the old man was in his grave, his secret buried with him, — which, however, his greedy relatives were trying to discover, by systematically demolishing the old house; when, one afternoon, as Phronie was passing through the back shop, she suddenly stopped, fixed her eyes on something, advanced, looked still more closely, and uttered an exclamation.

"Ma!" she called. "Do come here!"

"What is it?" her father inquired, looking

up from a thin sheet of cake which he was covering with jelly.

"Lem's coat," she exclaimed. "Do you know what this is?"

"I don't see as it makes any difference what it is;" and after a glance, the baker returned to his jelly-cake.

Neither did Mrs. Wilbur, who came in from the front shop, perceive any significance in the girl's discovery.

"Don't you know?" she cried; "it is the coat he used to wear about the bakehouse; he had it on, the evening of the robbery, and he hasn't worn it since. He wears his other coat when he drives the wagon. And this — and this — don't you know what these things are?"

She was growing more and more excited; her mother stooped, lifting the coat-sleeve toward her eyes, and picking at the specks Phronie pointed out.

"Some sort of seeds — not thistledown," she ventured.

"Don't touch one of them!" cried Phronie. "They are milkweed seeds. Andrew had some pods in his pocket, and they got smashed when he was robbed. See! they are nowhere but just here on the cuff!"

"Even on the inside edge of the cuff!" Mrs. Wilbur exclaimed, beginning to take in the serious import of what seemed at first so trifling.

"Lem was in the shop when the robbery took place," said the baker, looking scowlingly at the seeds.

"You don't know that he was," his wife replied. "You were not there yourself. He was there *after* the robbery, for he changed his coat, and went out the front way, just before Andrew came in. Phronie remembers that."

"Better say nothing about it. Let the coat hang there," said the baker, rolling up his cake. "It may lead to something, though I don't believe it."

"Andrew used to carry his road-book — and the money, when he had any in bills — in that pocket," said Phronie. "Lem knew it; and Lem knew he was going to collect bills that day."

There were only five seeds, with their feathery attachments, on the coat cuff. There were, however, other bits of down from which the seeds had been broken off. Mrs. Wilbur, as she examined them, took on her daughter's excitement. Phronie brought one of the fresh pods Andrew had sent her, opened it, and pulled off some of the seeds, for comparison.

"Sure as you're a live man, Thomas Wilbur," her mother exclaimed, "that cuff has been in Andrew Hapnell's pocket! It's a clue! Thank Heaven, at last we have a clue!"

Suspicion had already fallen upon Lem; but bad as were his habits and his associates, it was hard to believe that he would be guilty of so bold a robbery. Now, however, even Mr. Wilbur's obstinate opinions were shaken.

"And I believe Ike knows something about it," Phronie declared. "There's been something between him and Lem for a long while, that I couldn't understand,—and they've been thicker than ever lately."

"I've noticed the same, now I think of it,"
said her mother. "Leave all to me, now, and
we'll unravel the mischief."

Accordingly, when Ike came in, she collared
and accused him.

CHAPTER XXVI.

IKE protested his innocence, but appeared so
thoroughly frightened that Mrs. Wilbur felt
sure some valuable information might be shaken
out of him.

"It ain't anything about the robbery!" he
whimpered. "It's about — about — you remember when Dicky lost flesh last summer?
Lem bored holes in his manger, so the grain
that we fed him would run through faster'n he
could eat it. There's a dark corner there, and
a box where we used to have a setting hen.
The grain run into the box. But I found out
the trick one day, hunting hens' eggs.

"Lem said he'd have my scalp if I told ; and
after that he used to hire me to go and pull the
hay out of Dicky's rack, and put it into the
General's, when he couldn't get a chance to do
it himself. After Towner took Dicky. Lem

165

plugged up the holes, and he didn't dare bore any in the General's manger. Said he was bound, though, to have Andrew put out of his way."

After this confession wrung from the boy almost sentence by sentence, Mr. Wilbur took him to the barn, and ordered him to point out the plugs in the manger.

"He's the biggest scoundrel that ever lived," he said, "or else you are telling an abominable pack of lies!" But there were the pegs, not too carefully trimmed off, and the box beneath, with some oats still in it, not wholly shaken out of the hen's-nest litter.

Mr. Wilbur proposed to put this new evidence at once into the hands of the police, but his wife restrained him.

"You were too hasty with Andrew," she said. "Now don't be in too much of a hurry with Lem, and spoil everything."

He took her advice ; he waited till Lem came in at dusk, then said to him, quietly, "Whose coat is that hanging there, yours or Andrew's?"

" Mine," said **Lem.   He was a** little surprised
at the question, since the baker had **seen him**
wear **the** garment a hundred times.

" What makes you leave it here ? "

" I don't know.   **I just had it to** put **on when**
I was **at work** about the shop."

" **How** long since you **wore it ? "**

" Not since I've been driving."

" That is, not since that night ? " **said the**
baker.   " **Look** at the cuff **of** the **right sleeve,**
and see what that stuff is sticking **to it."** He
had turned from whatever work he **was doing,**
and stood sternly watching the driver.

" Blamed if I know ! " said **Lem,** holding **it**
toward the gaslight. " Cotton, **ain't it?** Or
dandelion down."

" How did bits of cotton, **or down of any**
kind, get on your coat cuff?" **Mr.** Wilbur
grimly demanded.

" I don't know **no** more'n **the man in the**
moon," replied Lem, pale and disturbed.

" **I** know ! " said the baker. " That's milkweed down, and you got it out of Andrew Hapnell's pocket.   Don't you pick it off ! " he thun-

dered out. "Not till the police have seen it. Your game is up, Lem Gorbett!"

Lem stood aghast in the gaslight, quite dumb for a moment, then faltered out, with a sickly attempt at a smile, —

"You don't think — I " —

"I don't think at all!" struck in the baker. "I know! Everything is out, or coming out, even to your boring holes in Dicky's manger, and starving him, so that I would put you in Andrew's place. A man that can do such a thing as that to a dumb beast will be guilty of any crime he thinks for his advantage. Don't you lie to me! Tell me anything but the truth, and I turn you over to the police in a minute."

Lem was so overwhelmed by this torrent of terrible accusation that he did not try to speak at all. He stood glaring and grimacing with fright, and breathing quick, short breaths.

"The only chance for you," said the baker, "is to tell me everything this minute, and return that money, or give me some reasonable assurance that it will be returned, and name

"'IT'S A CLUE!'"

your confederates. I'll **give you** just one minute to say '**I** will ' or '**I** won't.' "

Lem didn't wait for **the minute** to expire, but
muttered, "*I will !*"

"**Who** **were** the scamps?" the **baker** demanded.

"Ned and Sol Burge.   **But we didn't mean it**
for a robbery," said Lem, with trembling lips.
" **We just meant** to take **the money, so Andrew**
couldn't hand **it in, and** **you would lose** confidence **in him.**"

"Where is it now?"

" Hid in the barn, unless the Burges have got
it.   They are bothering now to have it divided,
though they **was** willing **I** should **keep it** hid
till the excitement **about it blew over.** They
wanted to drive him out **of town, for fear** he
would **get old** man Petridge's money, or prevent them from getting it."

In his shaken condition, Lem was willing **to**
tell everything ; he even charged **Sol Burge**
with being the cause **of the** General's running
away from **Andrew** in **the** summer (by putting **a** thistle under the horse's tail) ; **and he**

offered to go at once to the beam in the
barn, behind which he had hidden the
money.

"I meant to get it before, or have Ike pretend to find it, and make you believe Andrew
had put it there. But his going away spoiled
that plan; for, of course, if he had meant to
steal it, he would have managed to take it with
him."

Lem further declared that it was not he who
took the road-book from Andrew; he had indeed put his hand in the pocket where he expected to find it, while the Burge boys held
their victim, but it was Sol who then tore open
the buttoned coat, and found it.

CHAPTER XXVII.

GREAT was the joy of Phronie and her
mother over Andrew's vindication; but to render their triumph complete, he should have
been there to share it. And he had gone off,
no one knew whither, with his burden of cruel
wrong.

The next day's issue of the evening paper,
in which Andrew had read that entertaining
paragraph about himself, had another item on
the subject from the same lively pen. It began
with the statement that the question, "Was it a
robbery?" had fortunately been answered in a
way to relieve young Hapnell of all suspicion
of fraudulent design.

"*Hapnell*, it seems, is the correct rendering
of the name, and not *Happenill*, as our misin-
formed reporter had it. Perhaps *Happenwell*
would be a more appropriate orthography for

171

our little romance." For a little romance it
proved, in the hands of the fanciful writer,
with Andrew for its hero.

Alas that the hero could not have had the
satisfaction of reading also that pleasant sequel
to the first harrowing chapter of the tale! But
he was that afternoon far out of reach of Boston evening papers, travelling a lonely country
road in Western Massachusetts.

He was weary and discouraged; he had been
tramping all day in search of work, and had
had nothing to eat since morning. He was literally out of money, having spent his last cent
for his last night's lodging and a meagre breakfast

Nobody seemed to want the services of a boy
like him, and he had no trade by which to
recommend himself. He was not even acquainted with ordinary farm work. He might
have assisted at gathering apples, but it was not
an apple year, and other crops were all in.
There seemed to be nothing doing in the sleepy
villages he passed through; he could not even
get a job of sawing wood.

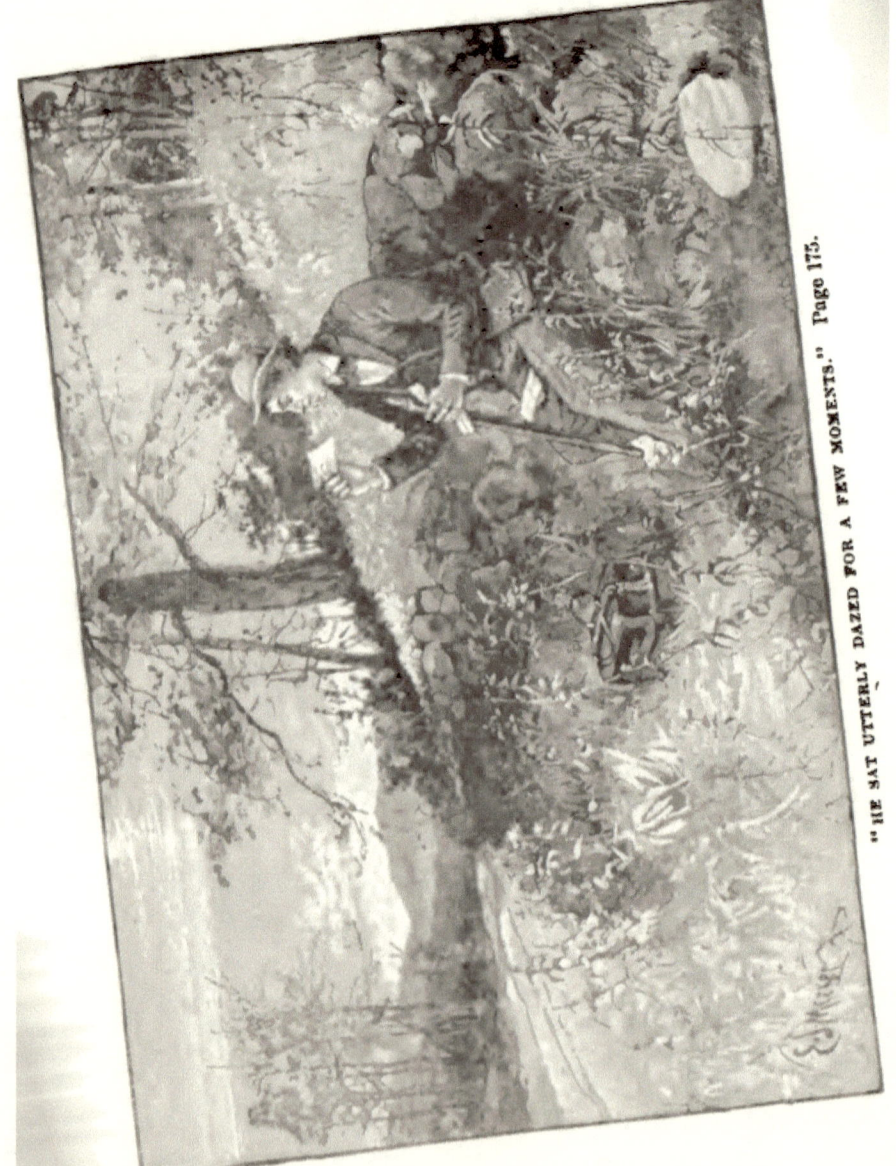

"HE SAT UTTERLY DAZED FOR A FEW MOMENTS." Page 175.

What was he to **do for** supper and **a** night's
lodging? He might crawl **under a** stack after
dark, but he could not **eat** straw. **Was it** possible that he, Andrew Hapnell, would be reduced to asking for **bread,** like the tramps **who**
had so often stopped to beg at his mother's door?

"**It** can't **last** always," he said to himself, as,
haggard, hollow-chested and **footsore, he went**
stooping under his burden along the rough
highway. "**If I** can find **a village, I'll try to**
sell or pawn some of my things."

He carried his valise on his **back, slung on**
his cane, the **old man's** cane, which **he** had
found useful in his long and toilsome journey.

"There's one thing **I** should **like,**" he had
said on taking leave of the nephew in possession of the house, after Miser Nathan's death.
"That **old** walking-stick. **He gave it to me**
two or three times, but **I** don't suppose his
giving amounts to anything."

"Not unless **I** say you can take **it,**" the
dead man's nephew and guardian had replied.
"**I** don't object." He cast **a** contemptuous
glance **at** the clumsy cane, which somebody

had removed from the old man's side after
his death, and placed in a corner.

" You may not think I got to care for him, "
said Andrew; " but I did."

He now carried the cane slanted over his
shoulder, and his right hand, grasping it to
balance the weight at the other end, brought
the head down before his eyes.

" I follow it," he said, " as the donkey followed the carrot hung just before his nose.   A
piece of the frigate *Constitution!*   I might as
well be adrift with it on the broad Atlantic.   The
silver dollar given by Lafayette or somebody" —

A sudden thought struck him.   " If it's real
silver, I might at least turn that into money,
and eat it ! "   In the midst of his weariness
and misery, all sorts of fancies flitted through
his brain, and he was already thinking of something far away in time and space, — an incident
of his school days in Ohio, — when he found
himself mechanically picking at the ferrule.

It seemed tight enough, but there was a rivet
which could be pushed in ; and this rivet,
though evidently not silver, was brighter than

the ferrule it served to hold in place. It was of steel, and must have been kept bright by frequent rubbing. All at once Andrew's wandering thoughts were brought back by a startling discovery.

It was not a rivet, but a spring. He tumbled his valise against a wall by the wayside, and himself beside it, and, sitting on the brown turf, among the goldenrods, he eagerly applied himself to study the mechanism of the cane. Pressure on the spring enabled him to twist the head. Twisting the head unscrewed it. Off it came in his hand, while his other hand held, not a solid stick, but a tube, in which a roll of papers appeared.

There were, in fact, rolls within rolls. Picking at them with fingers and knife-blade, he pulled out the core of all, about the size of a pencil, and unfolded it to a handful of crisp, curling bank notes. Outside of these were strange-looking, printed sheets, which, drawn out and unrolled, proved to be government bonds, with their rows of coupons attached.

He sat utterly dazed for a few moments.

Then, as he slowly realized the incredible good fortune that had come to him, in the extremity of his need, a bubbling laugh began deep down in his heart, welled up, and burst, shaking him to a mere jelly of joy, and showering tears from his eyes.

Suddenly he gathered together the treasure in his lap, and looked quickly up and down the road, to see that there were no witnesses to his extraordinary conduct.

There was nobody in sight. The old man's long-hidden riches were revealed; if not millions, they were at least thousands, and there was no one to dispute with him their possession.

There were three bonds of a thousand dollars each, and one of five hundred. There were over two hunded dollars in greenbacks and bank notes; moreover, the bonds still bore the coupons due in November As the bonds were payable, interest and principal, in gold, and gold was then at a premium, the whole amounted to not less than five thousand dollars in current funds.

Andrew made a rapid computation to that effect, as he rolled up the bonds again with the bills, saving out enough for his present needs; and, returning the rest to the cane, he screwed on the head. Then, forgetful of hunger and fatigue, even of the wrongs he had endured, he took up his valise and tramped on, to command supper, lodgings, luxury, and conveyance to any part of the world, at the touch of the fairy wand he carried in the shape of a clumsy old cane.

Still it all seemed to him fabulous, more like an "Arabian Nights" tale than a sober reality. But his happiness — if the feverish excitement he felt could be called happiness — was marred by the intruding thought that this wealth was not altogether rightfully his; that to keep it safe, he must keep it concealed.

He reached a railroad station in about half an hour, and learned, to his satisfaction, that by waiting half an hour longer, beguiling the time with a good lunch, he could take a westward-bound train, and sleep that night in Albany, on his way back to his Ohio home.

CHAPTER XXVIII.

AFTER which, it seems strange that, only two days afterward, the recipient of this sudden wealth should have returned to the scene of his year's battle with fortune, from which up to that time he had seemed so anxious to get far and farther away.

He stepped from a horse-car as on the afternoon of his first arrival at old Nathan's house. He did not have his valise with him now; he carried only his magical cane. He walked up the street and over the hill, and smiled at the work of demolition going on.

" They were right in believing the old man had money," thought he; " but a little mistaken as to the place where he kept it."

He marvelled that Mr. Burge himself should have allowed him to walk off with the miser's cane.

178

A few minutes later Phronie uttered a scream
of joyful surprise at the sight of him walking
into the front shop.

"O Andrew, how glad I am! You have
heard the good news? Ma! ma! here is Andrew come back!"

Andrew stood gravely smiling, but somewhat bewildered, as mother and daughter
greeted and congratulated him. He did not
know what Phronie meant by the good
news.

"Has nobody told you, or haven't you seen
it in the papers?" Mrs. Wilbur inquired.
"How that money has been found?"

Thinking only of Nathan Petridge's money,
Andrew was confused, wondering if more hidden treasures had been discovered in the old
house on the hill.

"And how Lem has owned up that he and
the Burge boys took it from you?" Phronie
went on. "Don't you know?"

"I know it now for the first time," said Andrew; "though I suspected it before. I saw
the Burges ripping the old house to pieces,

as I came by. How happens it they are
at large?"

"Lem claimed that it wasn't meant for a robbery; and, as he owned up to everything, we
couldn't make up our minds to have them all
arrested," Mrs. Wilbur explained. "It was in
the papers, though, and I thought that must be
what brought you back."

"No," said Andrew, not half so much elated
by his vindication as might have been expected; "I've come to town on other business,
and I couldn't help looking in."

He was interrupted by a strong hand grasping his and squeezing it until he almost cried
out with the pain. It was the baker's; Mr.
Wilbur had left his work and rushed into the
front shop, stopping only to give his fingers a
preparatory wipe on his apron, the minute he
heard of Andrew's arrival.

"I haven't a word to say!" he exclaimed,
with more cordiality than Andrew had ever seen
in him before. "It was a shocking mistake.
But 'all's well that ends well.' Your place is
waiting for you, and I'm glad enough to see
you back."

"I didn't come for that," said Andrew, his strangeness of manner yielding to the grateful emotions that warmed his heart and brimmed his eyes.

The family made him stay for supper; and at table, with closed doors, he related the thrilling story of the cane. Even the baker, who had always before treated him with more or less surliness, listened with intense sympathy, and watched with eager curiosity while he unscrewed the head and showed how the papers were concealed.

"I had heard before of a miser's keeping his money in his cane," he said; "and I wonder I never suspected the old man. His little journeys away from home, I see now, were to get his coupons cashed, or a bill changed."

He had to pass the cane over the table to the baker, who examined it with astonishment and admiration.

"Now I must tell you," said Andrew, "what troubles me."

"Troubles you!" laughed Phronie. "I should not think anything need trouble you, after this!"

"But there does," said Andrew, carefully screwing the cane together again. "I want advice; I want to know what to do with this property."

"That's right! that's right!" said the baker, rubbing his hands and smiling blandly at their guest. Nobody was eating a mouthful. "You are not going to let a little money turn your head. You are not such a boy as that."

"Of course you won't spend it foolishly," said Mrs. Wilbur.

"MA! MA! HERE IS ANDREW COME BACK!"

CHAPTER XXIX.

HE IS FAVORED WITH SOME PRACTICAL ADVICE BY THE
FRIENDLY BAKER, BUT OBSTINATELY FOLLOWS THE
COUNSEL OF A VERY DIFFERENT MONITOR.

WITH a curious expression, as if the talk were
taking a different direction from what he expected, Andrew was about to reply, when the
baker, having taken up his knife and fork and
dropped them again, went on, —

"You see what our business is here, and how
much it can be increased. I'd like to enlarge
the bakery, build one or two more ovens, and
run two or three or half-a-dozen more wagons.
It could be done as well as not. And I'm free
to tell you now, Andrew, how well adapted I
think you are to the business. I never had a
man — let alone boys — I liked half so well."

"Though it took him some time to find it
out," Phronie couldn't help throwing in, with
a laugh.

"Now what do you say to putting your

money in here with me, having charge of the
outdoor business, and sharing the profits?"
cried the baker. "After due consideration.
No hurry about it. Your bonds are bearing
interest, and you can wait till you are a year
or two older — till you are twenty-one, if you
think best. But it's a good thing for a young
man to have an object in view, and to work up
to it. Meanwhile, the less you say about your
good luck the better."

Phronie looked to see Andrew's face light up
at what she regarded as a splendid proposal.
But his countenance was disturbed.

"You are very kind," he said. "I see how
much your business can be increased, and I
know I should like to have charge of the outdoor part of it. But this isn't just the matter
I wanted advice about."

His face was flushed, his features worked, he
passed his hand across his brow, and went on :

"When I first discovered that money, I was
in a frenzy over it. Mr. Petridge had told me
I should be his heir, and given me the cane ;
even Mr. Burge said I could take it. But then

I began to reflect. There was no question about the old man's insanity. Had he any right to dispose of his property? To prevent that, Mr. Burge had been made his guardian. I felt at first that I had got only what belonged to me. But does it belong to me?"

"In one sense it does," Mr. Wilbur replied. "Though I saw at once, if the thing was known, you might have trouble."

"Certainly, the Burges have no right to it," put in Mrs. Wilbur.

"It would be the worst thing in the world for those dissipated boys," added Phronie. "I think it has got into just the right hands, Andrew."

"I said all that, when I tried to reason myself out of my scruples," Andrew replied. "But there was something in me that wouldn't be satisfied. I thought I would go on to Ohio, and consult my friends there. But I knew just what my brother-in-law would say; he would say, keep it, and perhaps claim a share of it for my sister. He's just that sort of man. I asked myself, 'What would my mother say?'"

Andrew's voice was broken, and his face showed how deeply he had pondered the problem, and how much it had caused him to suffer before he made his decision.

"I knew too well what she would say," he went on, after a pause. "I was in Albany. I started twice to take the train for the West; but I couldn't do it. I was more miserable than I was before I found the money; and that convinced me I never could enjoy it. I said to myself that I was a fool to feel so about it, and I don't know but I am. But something controlled me; I had to come back."

Mrs. Wilbur wiped a tear from her eye. Phronie watched him with intense sympathy and wondering interest, laughing with bright tears in her eyes, as he told his strange story. Even the practical baker had to respect sentiments uttered with such deep and sincere feeling.

Mr. Wilbur ate very fast for a moment, then threw down his knife again, and asked: "And what was your idea in coming back?"

"I hardly know," Andrew replied, his voice

and countenance clearing, now that he had made his confession. " I felt that I must tell somebody who would take a disinterested view of the matter and give me good counsel. I ought to consult a lawyer; but I wanted to be sure of getting an honest lawyer, and I didn't know where to go for one. Then it occurred to me that Mrs. Wilbur might tell me."

" I believe you are right, Andrew," Mrs. Wilbur declared. " And we know just the man for you — Lawyer Casey. Don't you think so, Thomas ? "

" If he's to consult a lawyer at all," her husband replied,— " why, yes, Casey will be a good man. But I hardly see the use."

" That's what I think now !" Andrew exclaimed, a smile breaking through all clouds and lighting up his face. " Merely putting the matter into words has settled it in my own mind. It is all clear to me now, and I feel perfectly happy about it."

" That's right ! " cried the baker, eagerly. " Let the lawyers slide. Say nothing outside

of this room. That's what you mean — that
you'll keep the money?"

"No," Andrew answered, firmly. "I shall
give it up."

"If you feel so," said Phronie, "I suppose
you must. But it seems such a pity that you
can't get some good of it."

"I've got good of it already," he replied,
cheerfully. "If I hadn't found it, I shouldn't
have come back here, and I might never have
known that that other trouble was cleared up."

"The robbery?" Mrs. Wilbur exclaimed.
"The idea of anybody's even suspecting you!"

Her husband had no taste for that topic; he
hastened to change it.

"If your mind is really made up," he said,
"then the best thing you can do is to consult
Mr. Casey. Something is due you for all you
did for Mr. Petridge the year you lived with
him; for your trouble in bringing back the
money; and for the assault on you by his
boys."

CHAPTER XXX.

ANDREW had not thought of putting in any claims of that sort; and yet if he could openly and honorably keep any part of the money, there seemed to be no reason why he should not do so. He accordingly went that very evening with Mr. Wilbur, to call on the lawyer at his house, and put the management of the whole affair into Mr. Casey's hands.

The next day he returned to his humble occupation of driving a baker's wagon, and was so happy in it that he cared little what sort of a settlement was made with Nathan's heirs. He was at first even a trifle disappointed when he learned how much that shrewd lawyer had succeeded in saving for him out of the contents of the cane.

"There's such a satisfaction," he said to Phronie, "in earning myself every dollar I have,

180

and building up my fortune, if I ever have one, solid and sound from the bottom, and biding my time, that I'm almost sorry to owe anything to what seems mere luck.   However," he added, with a laugh, "I shouldn't wonder if the five hundred will do me about as much good as it would most young fellows of our acquaintance. What do you think, Phronie?"

The Tide-Mill Stories

By J. T. TROWBRIDGE

Six Volumes. Cloth. Illustrated. Price per volume, $1.25

Phil and His Friends.

The hero is the son of a man who from drink got into debt, and, after having given a paper to a creditor authorizing him to keep the son as a security for his claim, ran away, leaving poor Phil a bond slave. The story involves a great many unexpected incidents, some of which are painful and some comic. Phil manfully works for a year cancelling his father's debt, and then escapes. The characters are strongly drawn, and the story is absorbingly interesting.

The Tinkham Brothers' Tide-Mill.

"'The Tinkham Brothers' were the devoted sons of an invalid mother. The story tells how they purchased a tide-mill, which afterwards, by the ill-will and obstinacy of neighbors, became a source of much trouble to them. It tells also how, by discretion and the exercise of a peaceable spirit, they at last overcame all difficulties." — *Christian Observer*, *Louisville, Ky.*

The Satin-wood Box.

"Mr. Trowbridge has always a purpose in his writings, and this time he has undertaken to show how very near an innocent boy can come to the guilty edge and yet be able by fortunate circumstances to rid himself of all suspicion of evil. There is something winsome about the hero; but he has a singular way of falling into bad luck, although the careful reader will never feel the least disposed to doubt his honesty." — *Syracuse Standard.*

The Little Master.

This is the story of a schoolmaster, his trials, disappointments, and final victory. It will recall to many a man his experience in teaching pupils, and in managing their opinionated and self-willed parents. The story has the charm which is always found in Mr. Trowbridge's works.

"Many a teacher could profit by reading of this plucky little schoolmaster." — *Journal of Education.*

His One Fault.

"As for the hero of this story 'His One Fault' was absent-mindedness. He forgot to lock his uncle's stable door, and the horse was stolen. In seeking to recover the stolen horse, he unintentionally stole another. In trying to restore the wrong horse to its rightful owner, he was himself arrested. After no end of comic and dolorous adventures, he surmounted all his misfortunes by downright pluck and genuine good feeling. It is a noble contribution to juvenile literature." — *Woman's Journal.*

Peter Budstone.

"Mr. J. T. Trowbridge's 'Peter Budstone' is another of those altogether good and wholesome books for boys of which it is hardly possible to speak too highly. This author shows us convincingly how juvenile reading may be made vivacious and interesting, and yet teach sound and clean lessons. 'Peter Budstone' shows forcibly the folly and crime of 'hazing.' It is the story of a noble young fellow whose reason is irreparably overthrown by the savage treatment he received from some of his associates at college. It is a powerful little book, and we wish every schoolboy and college youth could read it." — *Philadelphia American.*

Illustrated Catalogue sent free on application.

www.ingramcontent.com/pod-product-compliance
Lightning Source LLC
Chambersburg PA
CBHW020614030726
47497CB00007B/2229